Sex, drugs & Acton Town

by
Charlie Pills

ISBN 9798733328621 (paperback)

www.charliepills.com

Special thanks to nobody. I did this all myself. Only joking. Way too many people to thank. You know who you are. To the ones who have listened to me going on and on for years about this story I wanted to write. To the beautiful people who have helped me edit and market it, to the ones who gave critical feedback, I love you all.

TRIGGER WARNING

Do not read this book if you are a woke, cancel culture snowflake.

This book is highly offensive.

It was the 90's, and everything was offensive, yet no one was offended.

The past is not yours to delete. Our memories live on.

So please just put the book down and go be offended elsewhere.

For Steve

This book is dedicated to the '90s and all those who walked through the doors of the Redback Tavern, Acton Town, London W3.

1

'He's getting married! Fucking married!' I spurt out as I storm through the front door of Man Source Recruitment Services, my place of employment.

'What? Like married as in a church married?' says William Bentley, the Branch Manager.

'Well, I'm not sure it's going to happen in a church, but yes, they are getting married for real. He proposed, she said yes, date yet to be determined' my voice cracks with emotion on the last word and William looks horrified.

Not because he's just been told that the love of my life, Juan, had proposed to Bitchface Charlene, the whore he'd dumped me for 6 months ago, but because I'd just shown emotion. He can see I am ready to burst into tears at any moment, something I'd been doing a lot since I was dumped. William fails to remember his frequent bursts of emotional tears, depending on which boyfriend had cheated on him or dumped him.

'Let's go outside and die,' he offers as a way of getting me out of the office and away from any potential candidates that might walk in looking for work. Going out to die is William's way of saying let's go outside to smoke a fag, but only he can say fag, because he is one.

As I stand in the courtyard puffing on my Marlboro Lights, I contemplate how utterly devastated I'd felt when my flatmate had come home with the latest from the Redback Tavern. She'd bumped into Juan who had proudly declared his news. With the misery of every dumped female in the world, I burst into tears.

William looks stricken and slightly annoyed at my continued display of emotion.

'Look, Bree, I don't know why you're blubbering over that piece of shit. Must I remind you of the shit list?'

I nod miserably with a loud, snotty sniff, another disgusted shadow crosses William's face. I don't want to hear it, but also, I need to hear the shit list. It probably won't make any difference, but it's worth a try in making me feel better.

'One,' continues Willy as he holds up a finger.

'He said he'd go travelling around the world with you, yet when you bought a ticket to Australia, he told you he couldn't leave on that date.'

'Two, while you were in Australia waiting for him, he told you he wasn't coming due to work commitments and for you to sleep with whomever you wanted to whilst away, knowing full well this was his way of saying I'm going to fuck everything that moves.'

'Three, on your return from Australia, he dumped you for Bitchface Charlene and four, he just got engaged to Bitchface.'

'Oh, and five, I'm sure he's gay,' William thinks all good-looking men are gay.

I start to chuckle at William's last statement, and before we know it, we are laughing quite hard at how pathetic I am.

'What's it going take for you to hate him, Bree?' says Willy kindly. 'Kill your family?'

I stop laughing and go back to feeling sorry for myself and continue to smoke.

'What you need darling is a night out on the town. Get under someone to get over him, it's been too long and life is way too short.'

William is right. I haven't done much since Juan dumped me, and I've also been poor as fuck since getting back from Australia.

'Yeah, that's an idea, though not sure about getting under someone, maybe a night on the piss would be good.'

William has obviously forgotten that only four weeks ago I'd gone out on the town, well The Redback anyway and had pulled some lanky bastard that didn't end very well. Another story for sure.

'By the way, where's Jonny? It's 9.30!' I exclaim, not meaning to get him into trouble. William looks cross as he glances at his watch.

'Did you not see him over the weekend?' I say more jokingly than spiteful. 'Bree, you damn well know that I didn't see him. Now stop your shit-stirring,' says William just as playfully.

Jonny Rocks is our South African stud muffin and the newest member of staff at Man Source.

He'd claimed at his interview that he'd been an experienced Recruiter back in Cape Town. His reference was suspiciously unavailable when William had tried to make contact, and on Jonny's first day at work, it was screamingly obvious he'd never worked in Recruitment, let alone an office.

William had suspected Jonny's resume was faker than Pamela Anderson's tits. Still, because Jonny was gorgeous and possibly gay, he'd hired him without even consulting the owner of Man Source, Jodie-Lee Pike, or The Pikey as she is not affectionately known behind her back.

A real ball breaker who always has us on edge when she is over in the London office which, thank God, isn't very often.

Jodie bases herself in the Berlin office but still expects to be consulted on what is going on in the Acton branch. She was not happy to hear Willy had hired without her approval. Her displeasure disappeared within seconds of meeting Jonny on one of her trips to London.

He is gorgeous and she was hoping to fuck him at some stage of his tenure at Man Source, preferably just before he left/got sacked so there would be no drama. She intended to start pursuing him once the company started winding down, something she was planning on doing within the next few months.

'He's running late,' says Willy defensively.

That's every day for the last 2 weeks I think but don't say out loud. William is very sensitive when it comes to the golden boy. To be fair, he's totally shagable and I would have been interested if my heart weren't already broken in two.

'By the way, William, please do not say a word to the team, ok?' I plead, 'I really can't be doing with any more of their pity.'

William doesn't look impressed and knows he'll be telling at least one person in the office, maybe all of them and all within a couple of hours, and I know it too.

As much as I genuinely love William and happy with his very laid-back management style, he cannot be trusted with any gossip whatsoever.

'So, how did you find this all out?' enquires William. By now, we are both on the third cigarette and Willy doesn't seem in a rush to get back to his desk. I am going to milk the fact that William loves gossip of all kinds and avoid working for as long as possible.

Though he is the official Team Leader of Man Source Recruitment, he still loves to skive off whenever he can, and if Jodie isn't around, he does it often. He is good at his job and is also good at getting results with little effort.

The other reason Willy isn't in a rush to get back is to make sure I'm not going to get all emotional and start crying at my desk.

'Jess told me last night when she got back from the Redback.' The Redback is an Antipodean pub in the heart of Acton Town, a lively place where you are guaranteed a good time involving drinking copious amounts of their signature drink, Snakebite (beer, cider and blackcurrant squash mixed together in a pint glass), drugs of any kind and an almost guaranteed shag at the end of the night.

'She knew I needed to know but fuck me, it hurt to hear those words, William. Apparently, he and Bitchface were showing off her ring and everything.' The tears start to stream down my face and I just can't hold them in any longer.

'The only thing I'm surprised about in all of this sorry mess,' says Willy, 'is the fact you weren't at the Redback having a Sunday session. So unlike you darl,' says William.

I was so relieved I had changed my mind at the last minute about going. Not that I'd had a premonition or anything like that; no, it was because I was skint. I really didn't want to go to the Redback sober without a gram of coke in my pocket (my favourite poison) and enough money for a Snakebite or ten (my second favourite poison).

'Anyway, he might not go through with it,' I say hopefully.

William looks at me with eyes that seem almost sympathetic but also slightly incredulous.

'Look, Bree, as I said before, you need to get over the bag of shit and find someone else. What you need is a good shag, and all this emotional shit will be over. Go to the Redback this weekend. Fuck I'll even take you if it stops all this nonsense.' He is referring to the tears.

I am taken aback. William hates the Redback Tavern, having only been there once when he had first arrived in London from Sydney. Not just because he is gay and the Redback is the straightest pub in London but because it is full of beer-swilling, pill-popping Aussies and though he is an Aussie from the Eastern Suburbs, he believes he is nothing like the travellers who drink there.

'I didn't travel halfway around the world to hang out with bogan Australians' is one of Willy's favourite sayings.

I, on the other hand, love the place. I've always found it good fun.

'Ok, Saturday night it is then Willy, I expect you to pay, though.'
I say, testing him. He looks aghast. Probably at the thought of
spending his money. He was what we like to call in the business,
tight as a nuns 'vag'.

William is about to answer me with what I hope will be a' yes of
course' when Aggie, our German receptionist, pops her head
around the door to the courtyard where we've been smoking for
half an hour.

'Sorry to bother Villy, but Jodie has called from Berlin three
times; she is on the phone now' she is holding up 3 fingers and
her eyes are narrow as she looks at me accusingly.

William immediately throws his fourth cigarette on the floor and
hurries back into the office to speak to Jodie. He knows she'll be
in a strop for him not being at his desk when she called, though he
really doesn't care that much.

Jodie-Lee Pike had left Australia to go backpacking around
Europe and had fallen in love with Berlin, within days of arriving
in the edgy city.

Rumour has it, she'd started an affair with a bigwig German who
ran one of Berlin's largest construction companies. He was

smitten with this dark-haired beauty from Australia who fucked him better than the prostitutes he frequented.

To keep her where he wanted, he'd pulled some strings and secured her a lucrative contract, supplying construction workers to his company who were rebuilding Berlin after the Wall had come down.

Jodie had immediately enlisted her good friend William Bentley, who she'd grown up with in Sydney. The fact William spoke basic German also helped.

She'd paid for Willy to come to Berlin and after a night getting absolutely wasted, they'd come up with the controversial name of Man Source - In Your Face Recruitment for her new company.

Man Source Berlin had been so successful in its first year that she had needed to open a London office to cope with the number of workers required.

Man Source Acton was opened, and William was placed in charge of the branch, including recruiting the new Consultants that were needed to process the construction workers.

I had been hired with limited recruitment experience, but apparently I'd come across as competent and funny in the interview. I also have a plummy English accent, something William is crazy for. A few weeks after I'd started, he confided in me that my accent had reminded him of the late Princess Diana. As William adored the Princess and still cried over her, my employment with Man Source was guaranteed.

Agnitha Swartz, the German receptionist had been sent by Jodie from Berlin. They had met one night in a club called E-Werk. Jodie had recognised that her London office needed a German to help with the paperwork and had sent her to William, but not before fucking her brains out. Aggie loved pussy and this suited Jodie from time to time.

Next came Jonny Rocks. Pretty useless, but oh so pretty, and it also meant Willy had a distraction from his personal love life. He also lived in hope that one day he might just fuck Jonny, because he is sure that Jonny is gay.

My sole job at Man Source is to get the construction workers registered and sent to Berlin, it is easy stuff, and I get to chat to hunky men all day. The exact reason William loves his job.

If my heart weren't broken, I'd have had plenty of men to choose from, but as I was in mourning, I didn't notice and wasn't interested.

2

I had persuaded my parents to let me live in London with my best friend since High School Jessica, after she had left Uni (which I had dropped out of by the end of year 1). I had preferred to go to the university of life, or as my dad called it, the University of drop out.

At first, my parents had been horrified and totally against their only child moving to London, where god only knows what might happen. They had visions of me being raped or murdered or, worse still, marrying a commoner.

But after a lot of tantrum-throwing by my mother, I'd eventually moved out of home and into a shared house with Jess and what a time we have had.

Jess is my sensible, finished University, got a degree and fab job in the city friend. I have 9 months of a Business Degree up my sleeve which is still proudly displayed on my resume.

We live in a beautiful house on the border of Chiswick and Acton. Obviously, when anyone asks us where we live, we always say

Chiswick. Not that there is anything wrong with Acton, it's just Chiswick is slightly posher and when I say slightly, I mean shit loads posher.

We'd fallen into a pattern of drinking Thursday through to Sunday and exploring all the pubs in London, when we'd stumbled upon the Antipodean scene, and what a scene it is.

I'd thought Uni life was wild, but backpackers took it to the next level, and we were hooked!

We'd never met such a laid-back bunch of people, and the summer of '97 was probably my best year on earth, and then it got a million times better. I met Juan.

Dark, broody, tall and athletic, just my type! Though I have been known to fancy blondes and redheads, so I suppose my type really is just hunky men. It was instant lust at first sight for both of us.

Though Juan has Brazilian parents, his accent is posher than Hugh Grant's, and that's what I like the most about him.

His parents are Diplomats stationed in London, where he and his siblings attended school; however, he is so Brazilian in other ways, so foreign to me, and so intriguing.

He is an official backpacker, too, because he owns a backpack and has toured the world surfing. I was in awe.

We'd spotted each other across the bar at the Spotted Dog in Willesden Green. We had both been singing along to a rocking Oasis song and the connection was instant. Before the last orders were called, we were sucking face like there was no tomorrow.

He'd wanted to go clubbing and had invited Jess and me along with a group of his equally good-looking friends. It was on this night I took my first ecstasy pill and I literally had the best night of my life. And I lost 3kgs from all the dancing. Happy days!

Juan didn't invite me back to his place. I was disappointed and had secretly thought he must be gay. Apparently, he'd wanted to show he was a true gentleman and gentlemen didn't try and shag on the first day, but still!

Our second date was much more sedate. We'd gone for dinner at The Horse Bar and Restaurant in Waterloo. We had spent the night talking and really getting to know each other and by the second glass of wine, I knew I was going to sleep with him.

He was so damn perfect I had prepared myself for him being a crap shag or having a baby dick but I needn't have worried. He was hung like a donkey and fucked like a porn star.

14

The first time we fucked, it was hard and fast and over in seconds. The second time that night was in the shower, and he took his time, pleasing me and getting to know what I liked and wanted. The third time we fucked, well, that was pure filth!

We fell in love quickly and spent the next few months in a beautiful relationship. Something I had yearned for all my life and it was terrifying yet breathless all at the same time.

When Juan had started talking about going travelling with me and leaving his really good job, I took this as a sign that we were on our way to happily ever married with babies. So when I booked my flight to Sydney as a surprise and a way to make him actually do it, he had seemed shocked and really pissed off about it all and I was confused.

He eventually promised me he would come. A few weeks later he told me he would be changing the date of his departure as he had a few things to clear up and that he would join me later on in the trip and insisted I leave on the intended date, which I was reluctant to do. However, I'd bought the ticket and thought Juan would join me.

A month into my very lonely trip around Australia, waiting patiently for Juan to join me, he eventually admitted over the phone that he couldn't possibly join me. He'd been promoted at work and now was not a good time to go travelling.

He again encouraged me to stay in Australia, to enjoy myself and to finish the trip. I had permission to screw whoever I liked and that he'd be waiting for me on my return. I was gutted.

In a blind panic to get back to him, I rushed my trip up the east coast, not really enjoying myself or appreciating where I was, just hell-bent on getting back home. I had a very uneasy feeling.

I arrived back in Heathrow eight weeks after leaving the UK, to a cold and miserable day and called Juan before I'd even bought my Tube ticket. The minute I heard his voice, I knew something was very wrong. He was cold and not at all excited to hear I was home. He sounded angry to hear from me.

He said he'd call me later once I was settled in. We could talk then and not to bother coming to his place as he was busy, so I went straight to his flat with the hope that once he saw how tanned and gorgeous I was looking, he'd shag me right there on the doorstep.

When Juan opened the door, he looked shocked and scared, and as I tried to kiss him, he pushed me away and said the words I had been dreading but somehow knew were coming.

'Bree, sorry mate, I met someone else, and she's living here with me now, you'll have to go.'

And just like that, my world fell apart. I burst into tears from the shock, and I think at one point I was on my knees, begging him to take me back. Not my finest moment. I left after a while when it was clear he wasn't going to take me back.

There you have it, my sorry, miserable story about the love of my life who has just declared he's marrying Bitchface Charlene.

So, who is this Charlene, and what is it she has that I don't? Well, she's thinner than me (bitch), richer than me (fucking bitch), but does she suck cock as good as me? I don't think so.

She's a rich South African princess (not a real one) who has stolen and tricked my man and I'm going to win him back. I have a plan and I've written it down to make it official: -

1. Get thinner – easy to do, must snort more coke and only drink vodka. Avoid food where possible.
2. Get rich – not sure how, but I might combine my love of cocaine with selling it. Will speak to the dealer about joining his team. I can't see anything going wrong with this plan: Except for potential jail time, snorting all my

product or getting killed by the Acton mafia for taking over their patch. A small price to pay for love.

3. Remind Juan I give the best head ever (his words, not mine).

3

Back in Johannesburg, before leaving for London, Charlene's parents could not stress enough the importance of obtaining a British passport by any means possible. Now in the late 90's, even after the rainbow nation has been formed, they know this honeymoon period of peace will not last and they want their children out. Whilst South Africa is a beautiful country with many positives, they believe it is only a matter of time before crime explodes. Charlene comes from a wealthy and upper-class family residing in the exclusive suburb of Sandton, but they still live behind tall fences, with bars on the windows and guard dogs patrolling the grounds of their property. Getting out of South Africa is the goal and marrying their only daughter off is their way out.

Now, Charlene lives in a house share in Wimbledon, with another friend of hers from SA. She is happy to be sharing the space with other South African girls who come from the same standard of living as her. Yes, they've all had servants back at home, but they are independent women who keep their rental spotless and expect all guests to comply with their rules.

On her first week in London, Charlene registered with all the usual city recruitment agencies. She was snapped up when she tested at 70wpm on her touch typing and advanced on all software packages and was placed at an international head-hunter service as the Department Secretary for a four-month contract. Her starting hourly rate is £10, which, when converted to South African Rand, is R100. She felt rich and successful, and her parents were over the moon that she'd landed on her feet so quickly.

Charlene had left South Africa for one reason and one reason only, to bag herself a rich British husband. Her radar had been working overtime for the last few weeks since arriving in London, and Juan did not stand a chance. She would be his Secretary as well as supporting two other Associates, and while Charlene didn't care too much for the other two, she was instantly attracted to Juan. His handshake, which seemed to go on for minutes, not seconds, convinced her he was attracted to her too.

Charlene dressed for success but also wore clothes that accentuated her ample figure. Tight white shirts, see-through enough so you can just make out her saucer-sized nipples attached to her double D breasts, and skirts short enough to still be classy for a corporate office whilst showing off enough leg to be deemed acceptable.

Every morning Charlene comes into the office wearing yet another amazing outfit, always popping her head into Juan's office to let him know that she has arrived and asking if she can make him a coffee. Juan always said yes and usually followed her into the staff kitchen to chat. He loved to watch as her tits bounced slightly as she moved, and when she bent down to pick up something she had dropped, which seemed to be often, he sometimes got a glimpse of her knickers. She wears brightly coloured knickers, and he has decided pink is his favourite colour.

Charlene worked out early on that Juan wasn't married. However, he did have a girlfriend. His family are wealthy Diplomats and landowners back in their native Brazil. She is also smitten with his plummy English accent. She decides that he will be the one she marries, and she hatches a plan.

She starts by being the most amazing Secretary ever and Juan and the other associates are impressed. She wears her outfits and she hangs on every word he says, making him feel important. She makes his coffees, just how he likes, every morning without fail and always arrives with a bounce in her step and a smile on her face and before long, she knows that Juan is interested in her. Once he became a bit flirty with her, she knew it is only a matter of time before they would get their opportunity.

That opportunity came quicker than expected. One of the other team members was having goodbye drinks at the local pub just around the corner from the office and the whole team were invited. Charlene ensures she is wearing a low cut, tight top and tight skirt with makeup just subtle enough to make her look gorgeous.

Charlene and Juan find themselves talking to each other for most of the night, drinking their drinks and getting quite tipsy, though Charlene makes sure she doesn't get too drunk as she wants to come across as ladylike. By the time last orders have been rung, they are the only 2 left from the team and as they leave the pub, it feels natural when Juan leans in for a kiss goodbye and they end up snogging. He asks her if he can come back to hers for coffee and she says yes, but only for coffee. Juan knows otherwise.

They don't drink coffee when they get to her house, they fuck, and they fuck good. Charlene pulls out all her tricks to make sure

Juan has the best night of his life. On his way home the next morning, after having mind-blowing sex with Charlene in the shower before leaving, he thinks back over the night and can't stop smiling. She had asked about his girlfriend, but he had shrugged it off and implied the relationship was over anyway. He'd cheated on Bree a few times, but this was something different. He couldn't get Charlene out of his mind and was excited to get back to the office on Monday with this secret that they now shared.

Their clandestine relationship continued and they tried hard to hide it from everyone at work. Still, most were suspicious of the two due to all the late working nights. Charlene knows that they are beginning to fall in love and she starts to push for him to leave Bree, take a leap of faith and be hers.

It was natural for her to move in with Juan the day Bree left for Australia. Though unexpected at the Redback of all places, the proposal was a given because she knew Juan couldn't get enough of her and knew they were compatible both in terms of wealth and education. She had won, and though her husband to be wasn't born in the UK, he held the passport, which was good enough for Charlene and her parents.

4

Jonny Rocks, the man, the legend, and Man Source's newest recruit, is running late for work again. And this time, he is stressed about it. Not much stresses Jonny, but he knows his time at Man Source is numbered if he continues to take the piss.

He knows William has the hots for him, as does Jodie, but he also knows this will only get him so far, and he's almost reached so far.

'Fuck,' he mumbles under his breath as he checks his watch and then checks which station he's just arrived at. Hammersmith. Still four stops before Acton Town and then it's a 15-minute power walk to the office. 'Fuck!'

And the reason for his lateness can still be smelt on him. His cock moves slightly at the thought of her and he quickly pushes it away as a boner on the underground just isn't acceptable.

He'd reluctantly gone to the pub with a few of his flatmates last night, not really wanting to have a mad session on a Sunday, especially as he was completely hungover from the night before. But his roommate had been very convincing.

He was happy he'd decided to go to pub because he'd met the crazy bitch that had fucked him to within an inch of his life. It took all of his power and thoughts of Nana to stop his cock from rising up here on a packed Piccadilly train on its way to Heathrow.

His whole body hurt, and not all in a good way. Carpet burns on his knees, bite marks on his neck, scratches down his back and a knob redder than a clown's nose.

It had been great but not worth losing his job over. 'Bollocks,' he mumbles under his breath for the 100th time, much to the annoyance of the women sitting next to him until she lays eyes on him. Blonde hair, piercing green eyes and a smile that ripped your clothes off and licked your pussy all at the same time.

He got away with a lot because of that smile and he got what he wanted too, and he knew how to use it to his advantage.

Jonny had been a jobbing barman back in Cape Town but had decided to leave it all behind for the bright lights of London and he hasn't looked back.

He'd managed to land himself a great job as a Recruiter, with no experience (though his resume said otherwise), and he was raking in the money. Life was good, and he didn't want to fuck it all up for a great fuck.

As the Tube pulls into Acton Town, Jonny says a prayer of thanks, jumps off as fast as he can, runs up the stairs with relief and towards the barriers and out onto the road.

As he sprints out of the station towards the High Street, he starts to slowdown as he notices the hot chick with bouncy boobs walking towards him, and he gives her one of his come fuck me smiles. She ignores him.

'Now that's a girl I'd love to fuck,' says Jonny to no one as he continues his sprint to work.

5

I walk back into the office, having smoked four cigarettes one after the other and cried a bucket load of tears; I am trying to convince myself I am ready to work when really all I want to do is cry and talk about Juan and how to get him back.

I need to work out my plan, but today isn't about planning; it is about feeling sorry for myself, getting as much sympathy as I can possibly get and hoping to avoid all kinds of work.

I decide the team needs to hear my tragic story. I am also in need of some reassurance that everything will work out for Juan and me; I know William is the last person to approach, so I think I'll try my luck with Aggie. As she's partial to pussy she can be quite a man-hater and that is precisely what I need right now.

She's quite a petite and pretty young thing, and the men that come in here just love her until she opens her mouth and cuts them down in flames. Dare they try and flirt with her, she gives them 'the look', which can turn a man to stone.

She loves staring at my tits when I talk to her, but I'm too afraid to point out where my face is.

I go up to her desk at the front of the office by the main door, seeking comfort and reassurance. She listens to my sad story, but instead of words of comfort, I get a barrage about how Juan is a dirty pig who deserves to have his testicles ripped off and she knows someone who can arrange it.

'Is easy for me to arrange,' she says sincerely. I decline her generous offer.

'If you change your mind, just vink, and I arrange,' she says gleefully. Aggie terrifies me and most people that meet her.

Having not received any fluffy reassurance that Juan and I were sure to get back together, I reluctantly go back to my desk, feeling even more depressed than before.

I am just about to call my flatmate Jess, at work, to have yet another cry on her shoulder when the ever so late but oh so delicious Jonny Rocks walks through the door and I know he'll give me what I need.

'Hey, gorgeous girl, how's Bent Willy?' he gestures to William, who is still on the phone with Jody. Bent Willy is the nickname that Jonny has given to him, obviously behind his back, and it has stuck. No way could we say it to his face though, he'd probably fire us on the spot.

I giggle slightly at the name and then promptly burst into tears. Unlike Willy, who looked horrified when I had shown emotion, Jonny walks around to my side of the desk and gives me the biggest hug.

'Uck bru, don't cry, what's wrong?' his kindness makes me cry more until I start to feel slightly uncomfortable at this gorgeous guy being so close to me. I pull away shyly.

I then tell Jonny everything and he makes all the right noises and facial expressions, unlike Aggie and Willy.

'So, you see, I need to win him back. Until he says I Do, I feel I still have a chance,' I finish.

Jonny looks sympathetic to my situation and looks sad for me. 'What you need is a plan, my china.'

'Yes, exactly!' I squeal, feeling hopeful for the first time since receiving the news. Even Jonny thinks I need a plan to win him back.

'You're a player Jonny, what do I need to do?' I say to the slightly smug Jonny who wears that badge of honour with pride.

'Do what?' says Willy.

We hadn't noticed that his phone call to the Berlin office had ended.

'I need a plan to win Juan back, and Jonny said he'd help me,' I say excitedly.

They both look concerned.

'Bad idea,' says Willy. 'Um, when did I say I'd help?' says Jonny.

But before I can respond, a group of construction workers walk in looking for work in Germany.

My working day on this cold Monday, February morning in Acton Town has just begun. 1 hour and 45 minutes after I'd first walked in.

6

'Gather around team, I have an update from Jodie,' says William to us all once all the job seekers have been processed and ready to be sent to Berlin for a trial shift.

Man Source has a good system in place for both owner and candidate. If you can prove you have a trade and or/experience within construction, have medical insurance and a passport, you are almost guaranteed a job on one of the Man Source sites in Berlin.

The candidate must make their own way to Berlin, but once there, you make your way to Oscar Wilde Irish Bar in East Berlin, where Jodie will be waiting to 'induct' you into the company.

This usually means getting pissed and taking whatever substance you can get your hands on. Jodie does not mind what you do if you turn up for work on Monday.

Accommodation is provided for the first week in a local hostel, but it is up to you to source your own digs after your first payday.

If you fuck up or can't do what you say you can do, you are let go, so is the paid accommodation, and you are left with the outstanding bill. Only a few have ever been let go on their first shift when it was clear they had absolutely no idea what they were doing. Still generally, we, as Recruiters, get it right.

'So, Jodie has secured a further two shutdown projects in the east, ramping up in approximately four weeks. This is going to require major manpower,' continues Willy.

I stare blankly at William, watching his mouth move but not really hearing him. I am too busy seething about Bitchface.

Jonny is busy taking notes, something William had suggested he do at the beginning of his employment, due to his complete lack of knowledge of recruitment and his inability to remember things.

'So, the aim this week is to register anyone who walks through that door and I need you all to get onto the database and start calling up the candidates who are yet to be processed. Let's get these numbers up and make Jodie proud of us.'

We all collectively groan at William's use of words. Really? Proud? Who gives a fuck, is what I'm sure we are all thinking?

He stops talking and looks at us all, expecting questions. We don't have any.

Aggie doesn't look at all interested, and I look ready to cry at any moment, counting down the minutes until I can head to the pub and have a much-needed drink.

We all agree with William and saunter back to our desks to continue the day and get it over with as quickly as possible.

'So, my sunshine,' says Jonny, ever so lovely to me. 'Let's go out at the weekend and get you under someone, hey? What do you say, get over this wanker and stop these tears?'

I'm not sure whether he is being a genuine friend or semi-hitting on me, but either way, it is wholly welcomed from someone who looks like Jonny.

'Ok, Jonny, let's go to the Redback Saturday and find me a man to get under.'

Jonny winks a knowing wink but not before Willy sees it and looks thoroughly pissed off.

'It was my idea for the Redback this Saturday, Bree, and *I'll* be the one to find you a man,' says William jealously.

And with that, the clock strikes 5pm, and I'm out of the office quicker than a bat out of hell.

I've managed to persuade Jess to meet up at the Red Lion & Pineapple pub for a cheap dinner before going home. Much more economical than doing it myself. Two steaks and a bottle of red wine for £10 can't be bad.

The pub can be found on the corner of Gunnersbury Lane and High Street. It is known as the goldfish bowl due to its extra-large windows. It puts everyone inside having a drink on display to anyone walking past—a great place to have a drink just before going to the Redback.

'I still can't believe he's done this to me,' I blurt out the minute I see her waiting for me at our favourite corner table. By the looks of it, she's already finished a drink and a smoke.

'What happened, Jess? What did I do wrong? What is it that I didn't do? Cos believe me when I say I did everything that man wanted,' I continue.

Jess nods knowingly. Our bedrooms are next to each other. She hears it all. She knows.

'For fuck sake, Bree, I know you are hurting, babe, but I really can't listen to this shit tonight. I've had a shit day, and I want to eat, drink, and go home to sleep. Monday sucks.'

I am not hurt by her outburst; in fact, I feel somewhat guilty and agree to not talk about Juan for at least ten minutes while we eat our dinner and drink our wine.

'A bad day at the office, hey?' I enquire, having realised I haven't asked her about how she is doing as I'm totally consumed with my own pain and drama.

She is about to say something when something or someone catches her eye, and she is about to tell me not to turn around, but I do, and it is too late.

For a split second, I think she's seen Juan, and my heart starts racing, but with utter dismay I see its Lanky Bastard, the crap shag I had about a month ago. Fuck.

This was a man I'd hoped to never see again. In fact, he'd assured me he was off travelling around Mexico and had no plans on coming back.

Less than a month later and Lanky Bastard is again back in Acton. Double fuck. My mind is racing on how I can get out of the pub before he sees me, but it is too late. He has clocked me in the corner and looks as mortified as me. The cringe factor sets in once again and I want to die from the shame of it all.

Four weeks' previous I had gone out on a mad pity me session at the Redback, hoping to bump into Juan and hear the good news that he had broken up with Bitchface.

Juan didn't show up at all, which made me more miserable and made me drink more and snort more. I was messy as I stumbled around the dance floor, ready to make bad decisions, and Lanky Bastard turned out to be one of them.

We danced, we snogged, we did shots together, and at some stage it was suggested we carry on the party at the other great Aussie pub down the road, The Captain Cook. We carried on the party until sometime in the night when Lanky Bastard suggested we go back to his place which was only 46 seconds away. A great chat-up line he used often.

We chilled and smoked weed while we started to come down from the coke we'd been snorting all night. Actually, it was my coke we had been snorting all night and it was now all gone. Weed it was then.

And before you could say pass me a condom, we were naked and fucking for the Olympics.

As shags go, he wasn't bad, but he tried to force it up my bum at some stage, and that's when it all went tits up and the accident happened.

'Shitgate' is what Jess had gleefully named that night. I, on the other hand, had called it the worse cringe factor in living memory.

That isn't the worst of it though. It was how Lanky Bastard had reacted. He started to dry retch and gag and demand I get out of his flat.

I'd stumbled home and fallen asleep, waking with cringe factor and then shared the story with my flatmate, in the reassurance I'd never see him again. But here he is.

We finish our meal in record time, down a bottle of red wine in less than twenty minutes and head past Lanky Bastard, who by now is pretending he hasn't seen me, but I know he has by his ugly red face.

'Anal loving perv,' I quietly say as I walk past him.

Jess bursts out laughing and Lanky Bastard turns to look at us, embarrassed, knowing precisely what we are laughing at.

7

I've been thinking a lot about my relationship with Juan, especially the last six months leading up to my trip to Australia. It wasn't quite as perfect as I had imagined. The cracks had started to show several weeks before I'd left, but in my loved-up mind, I just didn't see it.

I can see it now, though.

And the more I think about it, the more it dawns on me that he was probably fucking Bitchface long before I left. I was so blind and blinkered, convinced, hand on my heart, that he was the one. Fuck, how wrong can one person get it?

About six months before the trip and 12 months into the relationship, my parents had invited us over to Surrey for the weekend.

Juan had met my parents several times and absolutely loved the oldies, and they adored him. Juan enjoyed our weekends away in the home counties and was always keen for a visit.

Mother had secretly bought 'the outfit' (the one she was wearing to my wedding), and Father had often spoken about the trust fund waiting to be spent on his only child's big day. He made no secret of the fact he was keen to spend it, as was I.

On one occasion, Juan had cancelled his trip to Surrey at the last minute, calling me late Friday afternoon to say he had to work all weekend and for me to go, something he'd never done before. I'd thought it odd at the time but went without him. My parents were disappointed but understood that work was important too.

In fact, there were quite a few weekends he had to work after that one. Fucker was probably balls deep inside the bitch.

The more I think, the more I seethe because I can see a lot clearer now, like I've been in a fog for the last few months. I see so clearly now I want to confront him and punch him in his smug, gorgeous face.

Jess said I am going through the normal phases of emotions for someone who has been recently dumped.

The first phase is weeping and self-pity. Well, I'd been in that phase for at least six months. Next came rage and revenge, exactly where I am right now. The next phase is acceptance.

I'm quite happy with rage and intend to stay this way for a while.

I remember when he said I was putting on weight. It was just a flippant comment one night after sex. But I was mortified and so I went to Plan C.

I didn't starve per se, I snorted so much coke for 7 days (Plan C) that I don't remember eating at all, and I went from a fat 54kgs (fucker) back down to 50kgs (stupid cunting fucker).

I am going to show this mother fucker what he is missing and never going to get back (revenge).

I'm going to the Redback Saturday night, and I'm going to look fabulous and very much like Jennifer Aniston (on half a gram, I *always* look like Jen), and I'm going to pull some stud muffin (no Lanky Bastard), and Juan is going to wish he is with me and I'm going to put two fingers up and say fuck you, Juan.

I like this idea, and it's what keeps me going through the week without so much as one tear.
Phase Rage, I love you.

8

Juan noticed Charlene's tits before anything else; it wasn't until later, when they were formally introduced, that he realised she had silky black hair, halfway down her back, toned and tanned legs that went up to a pert arse and the bluest eyes he had ever seen. But the tits, well, they were in a league of their own. Nipples pointed to the sky, at least a D if not more, and they bounce just enough to mesmerize as she walks into a room.

Charlene is the new temp that started in Juan's department, and she is there to support him and the other Associates. His department head hunts for large corporations in need of specialised talent. Juan's job is to track them down and negotiate employment outcomes by offering multiple benefits and usually extremely high salaries. He loves his job and loves it more now that Charlene has arrived.

Juan loves her body and loves the outfits she wears! He starts finding himself thinking about her on his ride to work on the Tube and wondering what she'll be wearing today.

He can't remember when he realised he liked her a lot, but his thoughts were only about her after just a couple of weeks. She mesmerized him, and he couldn't get her off his mind. They had fallen into a routine of having morning coffee and lunch together, and it was his favourite time of day.

It started to affect his relationship with Bree. As much as he loved her, she was beginning to get clingy and annoying. Recently she'd been going on about travelling, something he had been keen to do before Charlene. Now the thought of it just didn't appeal to him, but Bree wasn't getting any of the hints and kept going on and on about it. Her parents weren't much better, as they dropped hint after hint about marrying their daughter and making her an honest woman. It was beginning to piss Juan off, and he dreaded going to Surrey to see her parents.

Charlene made it clear quite early on that she was interested in Juan, and he made it clear that it was mutual. When the opportunity for them to get together came about, they jumped at the chance and continued to see each other on the side. Juan knew Charlene would expect him to leave Bree sometime soon, but she didn't push it, which he liked. He did feel guilty that he was cheating on Bree, but the more time he spent with Bree, the more he wanted out and to be with Charlene.

When Bree surprised him with her trip to Australia, he knew this was his time to strike. He was too scared to tell Bree that he wasn't coming and that he was in love with someone else, so he allowed her to leave; on the lie he would join her and had intended to send Bree an email saying she was dumped. Not a very gentlemanly thing to do, but he didn't care; he was in love with Charlene and only wanted her.

Bree had come back unexpectedly and he had been forced to dump her on his doorstep. He didn't like doing it, but he wanted Charlene more, so he had been brutal. It didn't make him feel good, but he had felt relief when Bree had left without too much drama.

Charlene gave Juan the best sex he had ever had and when he found out how rich her family were back in SA, it was a given that he would marry this woman. He loved her and believed their union would make a good one.

9

Apart from my rage, the only other thing that keeps me sane this week is the knowledge I will have a mad session at The Redback this Saturday, and it has gathered momentum.

William, Jonny, Aggie and Jess have decided to go, which means it is going to be an awesome night. I intend to get wasted and forget my woes. I'm also praying that Juan and Bitchface are going to be there. I really want to show off my skinny body and plan to wear my most revealing outfit, a cropped top and mini skirt.

The only upside to a broken heart is the broken appetite. I just can't eat, and the weight is dropping off me, which is fabulous as far as I'm concerned.

I love it when people say I am looking too skinny and gaunt. In my eyes, I can *never* be too skinny and gaunt. I just love rocking the Kate Moss vibe (body, not face).

This week at work, we have secured the number of workers Jodie needs to secure her contracts and she's impressed with our efforts and, for all her faults, she can be quite generous and has rewarded us with a £50 cash bonus.

This is perfect timing and I call my dealer to arrange the pickup of a gram of coke for Saturday afternoon, just in time for my jolly at the Reddy.

By the time Friday arrives, I feel almost like the old Bree again and haven't cried one tear in public over the shit bag. Life is slowly crawling back to normal.

Saturday finally arrives, and I am feeling excited and hopeful. Tonight could be the night Juan realises his mistake and begs me to take him back, or I meet the man of my dreams (for a second time), or I could just get a great shag. Win-win if you ask me.

The day goes well, and we do the usual Saturday stuff. Oasis gets played at full blast on the CD player as Jess and I potter around the house cleaning, before relaxing in the afternoon while watching TV and smoking a ton of weed. It is how we spend a lot of our weekends, and if we are particularly hungover, we rent out a whole series of Friends from Blockbusters and spend the day on the couch.

This Sunday will be no different. I've already been to Blockbusters this morning and rented Friends Season 3, ready for a day feeling like crap and watching the best show on earth.

I am thinking about tomorrow and wondering who is going to be on the couch with me. A shiver of horny anticipation goes through my body. I am ready to get laid. It has been a while.

I am waiting for my dealer to come over with the goods, and I've given him strict instructions not to deliver before 5pm due to the fact I know I'll snort the lot before I even leave the house.

My dealer, Acton's answer to Pablo Escobar, delivers 24/7. It is his unique selling point over all the other dealers. And his stuff is good. He is a good sort too and has often given me a gram on tick when I am skint, which is most of the time leading up to payday.

But tonight I am 6ft tall and bulletproof with a fifty in my pocket and a desire to spend it at the shop of Pablo. Jess has also put in an order for a gram and 6 pills. She likes her E's.

Pablo turns up at almost 5pm on the dot, almost like he has been waiting in his car outside our house, which later he said he had been. He knows how strict I am on delivery times, and he always wants to please.

It is Saturday night though, and this is his busiest night, and he doesn't have time to stay for long. He has been known to join us for a mini sesh if we have one at home but not tonight.

He does, however, have time to chop us both a fat one from his stash. The lines are so thick and so long it takes all my nostril power to get that baby up, but I'll be damned if I'm leaving even a speck behind.

As it hits the back of my throat, that familiar feeling of amazing comes over me. I know I now look like Jennifer Aniston, and the world is a fabulous place. Fuck I love coke.

'It's good shit,' says Pablo, a man of few words, but when he speaks, he speaks the truth.

We both give Pablo a hug and a kiss and a wee bit of tongue as a thank you, and he is off to his next customer.

'Hey Bree, you need any more, babe, I'm your man,' he winks,' and if you ever want to rent out your spare room, I have a friend arriving next week from Jeffreys Bay who needs somewhere to crash for a while and I don't have the room, just let me know, he's a surfer you know' and with that he jumps into his car and drives off.

My ears prick up when I hear the word surfer, and the thought of a gorgeous man living with us sort of appeals right now. I make a mental note to convince Jess it is a good idea, but that can wait till later. Tonight is upon us.

We snort a couple more lines, put our glad rags on, I had planned to wear a mini skirt, but the only one I own is so short it almost shows off my giblets! Jeans and a cropped top will do as it is winter. A little bit of blusher and mascara, and we are ready to take on Action Acton!

Once we are all glammed up and ready to go, we make our way out of Antrobus Road and onto the Tube at Chiswick Park; one-stop later, we are at Acton Town with a short walk up the road to The Mill Hill pub, our first stop of the night and where we are meeting the rest of the gang.

'How are you feeling about tonight? Are you hoping to meet Juan' asks Jess, knowing full well that was my hope/dream/plan.

'I've got my plan Jess and if he's at the Reddy, its 'operation win Juan Back' ok?' she looks stricken, especially as I'd been in Phase Rage for the last two nights.

'Or if I can't get him back, or he's not there, then 'Operation Get Bree Laid', ok?'

'That's the spirit,' giggles Jess as we walk through the doors of the Mill Hill and straight into Juan.

Fuck.

There he is in the flesh after all these weeks, looking the same. Ok, most people don't change in such a short time, but I'd been picturing him differently somehow.

I haven't seen him since my first day back from Australia, and that had been an emotional disaster. And it feels like years ago.

My stomach does such a massive flip, and my heart starts racing so quickly, I think I am going to be sick right there on the carpet.

He hasn't seen me as he shares a story with the boys at the bar. I stand transfixed for a second, trying to work out if Bitchface is with him. I'd never met her, but I know exactly what she looks like.

I'd forced Jess to recall every detail of her down to the colour of her eyes. Jess was so uncomfortable giving me this information, but I had insisted.

I need to know my enemy, my nemesis, the woman who stole my man so that I can plan and connive to get him back.

I need a drink and a line so badly, but both activities require me to walk past Juan.

Jess gives me a slight nudge, and the spell is broken. I start walking towards Juan, and as I do, he stops talking and notices me for the first time.

Concern flashes over his face, and I recognise the fear. Was I going to go crazy on his arse or slap his face or worse? He knows me well.

Instead, I act as if he is a dear old friend I haven't seen in years and it takes all my power to do so.

'Hey, Juan, how you doing, babe? Looking good, and it's been so long, hey?' I say as casually and as sweetly as I can muster. Fuck I'm a good actor.

He looks shocked but also pleased. He grabs me and brings me in for a peck on the cheek. His smell hasn't changed. Completely edible. Wanker.

'Hey gorgeous, it's been so long, babe, and so good to see you again. How you doing?' he sounds genuine and like he cares.

'Great Juan, you know me, always good,' I lie.

'Gotta go, I'm running late for a catch up with friends,' I wink with a knowing nod. Hopefully, he thinks I'm meeting a shag.

I walk off to the back bar, hoping his eyes are following my pert arse and I hold in my meltdown until I can at least get around the corner.

As I walk into the toilets, Jess follows me, and when we are safely away from everyone, I burst into tears and sob quietly on her shoulder. I don't have to say a word. She knows I am hurting badly.

It takes four massive, super fat lines of coke before I feel better and ready to face the pub and by the time we exit the toilets, Juan has already left.

Happy, relieved and miserable all at the same time. Mother fucking bastard.

10

I need another line and indicate to Jess I am going to the toilet.

'Off to powder your nose?' quips Willy as he sips his Bacardi and black, and the team do a collectively loud sniff.

'Fuck off,' I giggle, and off I go.

Seeing Juan has thrown me, as I wasn't expecting it. I had been hoping I'd see him tonight at the Redback, where I would have been prepared, but here at the Mill Hill has shocked me and put me in a spin.

A line of coke and a couple of large glasses of wine will help fix the shock. It starts to kick in as I head back to the bar. I'm beginning to feel my groove come back and I'm ready for a fabulous night at the Reddy.

'Come on, losers, let's get going; I want to go to the Redback now,' I say to Jonny, Willy and Aggie.

Everyone is still drinking their drinks and making small talk, but I'm in a rush, and my selfish, coked-up alter ego, has kicked in.

I don't care. I'm a supermodel, and everyone loves me.

After a bit of grumbling, mostly from William, who has been keeping an eye on a hot blond playing pool, I eventually convince them to leave.

'Bree, you owe me one babe,' is his passing shot as we head out the door into the cold Saturday night and up the slight hill and then right on to the High Street.

There stands the best pub in London in all its glory, The Redback Tavern. We link arms and sing Abba songs as we head towards the pub, feeling the effects of the drinks we have just skulled and coke we have snorted.

'Not for me, I like to be sober while I hunt,' said Aggie when I'd offered her a line earlier.

I'd also (reluctantly) offered Jonny and William one as well and had been over the moon when they had kindly refused my offer.

'I'm on the pills tonight, babe,' Jonny admits.

'And I have my own darl,' confesses Willy.

'Great news, my friends, and if I run out of coke or want a pill, I know where to come.' I say cheekily.

As the Redback comes into full view, we see the massive queue snaking up the building's side and almost at the greengrocers.

'Fuck,' we say in unison.

'Fuck, it's too cold to stand out here,' whines Willy, and I do believe he's about to jump in a taxi and go home.

But Jonny has a plan and tells us all to calm down.

'Follow me and watch how it's done, my chinas.' Fuck he's cocky, but you gotta love him.

We head towards the front of the line and the bouncers are staring at us with a look of 'no chance' on their faces, and the massive line of people are feeling hostile at our bid to jump the queue and get in before they do.

Jonny is whispering to the one and only female bouncer for a couple of minutes and before you can say fuck me sideways, we are being ushered into the Redback.

Some of the girls who had been waiting patiently at the front of the line start to protest, but the bouncer tells them to shut the fuck up.

I can't help myself as I turn to them and give them a 'I just got in cos I'm more important than you, and I look like Jennifer Aniston' kinda smile.

As we enter the vibrating and packed to the rafters Reddy, the excitement starts to pulse in my stomach, and I can see the rest of the crew are feeling the same.

'How the fuck did you manage that, Jonny?' I shout over the music.

'I have my ways, Bree. Just leave these things to the Rock Master,' he winks.

He later confesses to William that he'd fucked her a few times when he'd first arrived in the UK and she was looking for some action later, which he'd promised to do, for old time's sake and for getting us all in.

'Jonny, you are the man for taking one for the team,' says Jess and we all head towards the dance floor where Loony Tunes, the resident band, are playing Teen Spirit by Nirvana and we all declare it to be the best song ever. I have a feeling tonight is going to be a good night.

While everyone is dancing, I convince Jess to come do a walk around with me. I need to know if Juan is here.

We scout the place twice, which takes us a very long time due to the sheer volume of people. We don't see him or Bitchface. I'm disappointed because I'm ready to win him back now that I've got over the shock of seeing him earlier.

We find the rest of the crew up at the top bar to the left of the dance floor, where it's a bit quieter and gives us a great view of the place.

Trying to make small talk is hard over the noise, so we all just bop along to the music, drink our drinks, and smoke our cigarettes.

Jonny is the first to break ranks. He has been watching a blonde with big tits, dancing close to where we are standing, and he's about to make his move when the bouncer girl stops him in his tracks and starts whispering to him.

'Hey guys, she's on a break for 30 minutes and she's cashing in her favour. I'll be back soon, don't leave without me,' are his passing words.

Apparently, she lives upstairs, so they don't have far to go.

So that now leaves the four of us, and it's clear that Aggie has her eye on someone too.

'Come, let's dance,' she shouts to the rest of us and indicates she's off to the dancefloor.

A Split Endz song comes on and the crowd goes wild. The dance floor becomes a heaving, pushing mess, and I need to get off before I punch some fucker in the face.

Jess can see I'm getting wound up and suggests we go to the toilets by the cloakroom to powder our noses. I don't say no.

'Are you having fun' asks Jess as we wait in line for a cubicle to become vacant. Half of the Reddy has the same idea as us, and the line is moving slowly.

'I am, babe, but I'm just on edge. I want to know if he's here or not, with her,' I say.

I'm scared if I see her, I'll punch her, but at the same time, I want to be able to watch her and see how they are together. I want to literally torture myself!

It's our turn to get the next cubicle, and it can't come quick enough. We bundle ourselves into the tight space, and I proceed to chop up a couple of thick lines.

I cut up two fat lines each and we proceed to get them up our noses. I'm a pro and have been known to snort a line off a toilet rim. Not really something to brag about.

As we snake our way through the crowd towards where we'd left William and Aggie dancing, I quite literally smack face with Juan and my whole night changes, again.

'Babe, you're here; I was hoping I'd see you,' he says ever so flirtatiously.

I'm frozen. In happiness? In shock? And for a few seconds, I cannot say a word.

'Bree, Charlene's not coming here tonight; wanna go somewhere quieter for a chat or even a dance?' he says expectantly.

Instant rage as he mentions her name.

'Um, Juan, hey, as great as that sounds,' I say sarcastically. 'I'm gonna pass on it. I'm actually here with someone and he's waiting for me,' I lie.

I start to wave at my imaginary boyfriend, and Juan looks around to see who I'm waving at, but I get away before he asks me anything else, and I'm sure I see the disappointment on his face.

Fuck, now I really need to pull out all the stops and get me a man, but my heart is sore and my hope has been restored and I'm also a little bit raging from hearing her name. He wants to dance and talk to me. I can't wait to analyse the shit out of that, but it must wait. Right now, it is time to pull.

Jess has gone on ahead, and by the time I get back to the dance floor, she's pulled some short blond who looks Swedish, and I also spy Aggie pashing Tits that Jonny had his eye on.

That leaves Willy and me, but he's keen to go home and heads towards the door.

'I'm off home now, darl, see you Monday,' says Willy with a wink, and I'm sure I see him walk out with the pool playing blond from the Mill Hill. I will be quizzing him about it on Monday.

That is it, I must pull. Not just because Juan believes I'm here with someone, but because I've just watched two gay people pull shags in the straightest bar in town, and I'll be damned if I don't get one too.

And then I meet my Maori.

Tall, dark, handsome and covered in the sexiest tattoos I've ever seen. I do believe he's Maori. I've never shagged a Maori, and I see this as my opportunity to tick Maori off my list (I had been shagging myself around the world before I met Juan, my A-Z of nationalities). It is going well, having recently ticked off Scottish with Lanky Bastard.

After we kiss and smooch our way through a few songs whilst on the dance floor he suggests we go back to his flat for a smoke and a line.

He lives above Babylon Pizza Shop, almost opposite from the Redback, which is perfect because it gives me no time to change my mind.

As we walk towards the front door, I catch Juan staring at me from where he is standing and I give him a wave and smile. He doesn't return the gesture.

I decide that Maori and I should kiss passionately right there and then so that Juan has no doubt whatsoever what I'm about to go and do.

Two minutes later, we are in Maori's flat. I'm gushing about how I've never fucked a Maori and that I've always wanted to, whilst trying to ignore what a shithole of a flat he lives in.

Mountains of clothes cover his bedroom floor, ashtrays are overflowing, and beer cans are strewn everywhere. Ah, the life of a backpacker, I muse.

We snort coke, smoke joints, and start to fuck, and he fucks me good and takes his time. Sliding into me slowly and deeply before speeding up. He throws me on my face and fucks me deeply from behind, and he finishes quickly without going anywhere near my bum.

Once we've finished round one, we sit back and smoke the rest of the joint whilst propped up in bed. Sweaty from the sex and naked under the sheet.

'Bree, babe, you are good,' says my Maori referring to my sex skills. I know this already, but it is always good to hear it from the horse's mouth, so to speak.

'Thanks babe, you weren't bad yourself,' and I mean it.

'Hey Bree, I got something to tell you, babe,' Maori says quietly.

Fuck what now.

'I'm Tongan babe, not Maori, but you kept going on about your list, man, and you didn't really give me a chance to tell you hey,' he says, guilty.

61

I laugh at his awkwardness and reassure him it's ok. I apologise for making the cultural mistake. I make a mental note to put Maori back on my list and to tick Tongan off. Not that it had ever been on it up until now.

We finish smoking before Maori Tonga leans over to my exposed breasts and starts sucking on my nipple, making me wet and ready for sex again.

I'm about to climb on top for round two when the pile of clothes that had been on the other bed in the room starts to move, and a half-naked man sits up grinning at me.

'What the fuck, mate,' I ask angrily while trying to cover myself with the sheet.

'Hey babe, don't worry about him, Bree. That's just my roommate. He loves to watch, mind if he joins us?'

One second of contemplation before a massive resounding no, I get dressed, rant and swear and storm out of the flat and back out onto the cold, wet street.

And now I must walk home. Fuck fuckerty fuck fuck.

11

Today is Monday, and I fucking hate Mondays, especially after a heavy, quite disappointing weekend.

Yesterday, Sunday, I'd made my way home in the early hours of the morning back to the house after the Maori Tongan fiasco to find Jess going for it with the Random I'd left her snogging. All I wanted to do was tell her my news.

No chance of that as I listened to them riding each other. So I sat in the lounge smoking weed and drinking Jack, waiting for it all to be finished.

Our only bathroom is situated downstairs, through the kitchen and at the back of the house, which means they must pass me in the lounge at some stage.

I don't have to wait long. Random comes running down the stairs and looks embarrassed to see me sitting on the couch, staring. He's naked. He apologies for the lack of clothes and carries on to the toilet. I am impressed—no baby dick for this one.

Jess has heard us talking and makes her way down the stairs, thankfully in her dressing gown.

'Oh my god, I must tell you about my crazy night Jess' I blurt out, but she's not quite finished with Random and is keen to get it done.

'Have you got some coke left? I'm literally falling asleep while he's down there,' she indicates to her pussy.

I cut up four lines, and both Jess and Random have one each. I finish the last two.

'I promise when I'm finished, I'll be down to hear all the gossip,' says Jess as she's half-dragged up the stairs.

She never did come back, and at some stage, I fell asleep.

Once Jess gets rid of Random, we do what we do best on a Sunday. We watch Friends Series 3, smoke copious amounts of weed and gossip about our weekend men.

We manage to drag ourselves off to The Duke of Sussex, the closest pub to our house, later that evening and have a feed of steak and chips, a couple of pints of cider. We are both in bed and asleep by 8pm.

The perfect Sunday.

And now its Monday, and as I said before, I fucking hate Mondays.

I pick up 5 TNT Magazines from outside Chiswick Park Tube Station and make my way up Acton Lane.

At the top of the road is Man Source, opposite the library. I am not in the mood today.

The weather is cold and wet and as I walk through the door of Man Source, 10 minutes late, sitting at Willy's desk is Jodie-Lee Pike. The Pikey, all the way from the Berlin office, here on a surprise visit and she doesn't look happy.

In the words of Chandler Bing, could my day get any worse?

Motherfucker.

'Hey Bree, lovely for you to join us; hey, how you been doing, babe? Are ya surprised?' Says Jodie as sarcastically as she possibly can.

Her Australian twang instantly annoys me, as does her flakiness.

'Hey, Jodie, wow, what a lovely surprise' I lie and go in for the compulsory kiss and hug.

'Um, does bent, I mean Willy know you're here?' I ask, realising that he is late too.

'Yeah nah, totally decided to fly last-minute babes, just didn't have time.'

Lying bitch.

'So, are you, Jonny and Willy always late on a Monday?' she asks even more sarcastically.

The only one who has turned up on time is Aggie, and she doesn't really give a fuck whether Jodie is there or not.

Me, on the other hand, well I'm devastated. I had been looking forward to a day of digesting the weekend and talking about Juan. Did he mean what he'd said to me at The Redback? Did this mean he was going to dump Bitchface and beg me to come back?

Today is not going to be that day that I find that shit out and get to analyse it with the team.

I have no way of warning William and Jonny that the Pikey has landed, but Aggie quietly indicates that she's taken care of it, and I suspect she's sent them both a text.

Ten minutes later, William walks through the door as if nothing has happened and he's on time, five coffees in hand and five Gregg's sausage rolls.

William is a legend and knows Pikey can't resist a sausage roll from Greggs.

'Darling, I had a feeling you'd be in town today and looking as gorgeous as ever,' schmoozes Willy.

He minces across the office and gives her a massive hug and gives me a wink over her shoulder.

Bloody legend.

William can pretty much get away with most things, and Jodie always hangs out with William when she's back in London. I am hoping he takes her away from the office today so that I can get back to doing nothing.

They go to the courtyard to die and I sigh with relief as Jonny stumbles through the door, looking quite frazzled and severely hungover.

'Thanks for the text, babe,' he indicates to Aggie, who just grunts, and he sets about turning on his computer and making himself look like he has been in the office for hours as opposed to being 40 minutes late.

'Uck man, why today' Jonny mumbles. My thought exactly.

'So Jonny, how was she?' I enquire, and Aggie comes rushing over at the whiff of a good gossipy story.

Jonny proceeds very quickly, just in case Willy and Pikey come back, that he'd been up to his nuts in Security all weekend. In fact, he'd only just left her bed after getting the text from Aggie.

He is sore and his dick is throbbing once again, but he declares that she was worth it and he'd do it again in a heartbeat.

He also points out that we will probably all be able to jump the queue at the Redback from now one. He has literally taken more than one for the team. We are happy with this news.

Aggie doesn't want to share sex stories about Tits today; she remains tight-lipped. She must like her, I muse.

Me, well, I'm desperate to dissect everything Juan has said to me, but I don't get a chance as William and Jodie come back into the office having smoked half a packet of Marlboro Lights between them.

We have a team meeting, and Jodie gives us an overview of how the company is performing (excellently), how we are performing as a team (good but could do better) and what her plans are for the Acton Branch of Man Source.

'Jodie is there any chance of a secondment to the Berlin office at some stage,' asks Jonny quite bravely.

'I'm glad you've asked that Jonny and the answer is yes. I'd like all of you to come over at some stage this summer, especially as we get ready for shutdowns, but today isn't the day to discuss this. I'll get William to arrange closer to the time.'

A trip to Berlin is exactly what I need and I decide I'm going to hassle William to get this arranged once Jodie has gone back to Berlin.

After our coffees and sausage rolls, Jodie and William say they are leaving the office for a few hours as they have meetings to attend too.

We are thrilled and try not to show it. Today might turn out ok after all.

We watch them walk out of the office, wait 10 minutes just in case they decide to come back and then sit around my desk talking about our weekend and getting annoyed if anyone dares walk in looking for work.

I tell the team about Maori and they both laugh so hard I get pissed off, but eventually I see the funny side. I tell them about Juan and what he said.

'Do you think he wants me back?' I say, hopefully.

'Nein! He ist pig, das ist nicht so gut Bree' screeches Aggie.

I am not impressed. What the fuck would she know anyway.

I turn to Jonny, eyebrows raised.

'Bru, I think you must forget this man as he will only cause more heartache, my sunshine.'

I am also unhappy with his response, so I phone Jess at work, and we talk for over an hour like we haven't seen each other in months.

She thinks I still have a chance. I like talking to Jess.

'By the way, I'm thinking of renting out the spare room to Pablo's mate, what's your thoughts?' asks Jess as I'm about the end the call and go back to doing nothing.

'Yeah, cool, just make sure he's hot and likes to party,' I demand.

'Leave it with me, I have a plan' and she hangs up.

William disappears for 3 days and only returns to work on the Thursday. He's been on a 3-day bender with Jodie, and he is a super star in my eyes.

He also looks close to death when he eventually returns to the office.

'Never again. Never. Fucking. Ever again,' croaks Willy.

12

Jodie loves her trips to London and usually has a wild time with William. She has very few female friends, and that's exactly how she likes it.

After surprising the Acton Office on Monday and being thoroughly pissed off, though not surprised at how late everyone was, she started contemplating shutting down Man Source Acton earlier than planned. She doesn't like it when staff take the piss and the Acton team takes full advantage of her not being around to manage them.

William convinces her not to.

'Why chop your nose off, darl? Yes, they were all late. Big deal, I have it under control,' he says while they are drinking their coffees and smoking Marlboro Lights.

'We have an endless supply of workers who aren't jaded by Berlin life, so let's just make the most of that until you are ready to close shop for good,' he implores.

William is right, and Jodie knows it and Willy also knows that Jodie likes to throw tantrums and threats around from time to time; he can handle her.

Jodie is not in London just to work; she has come to get away from the crazy that has become her life.

Ever since setting up Man Source, her world has changed from poor, carefree backpacker to a millionaire businesswoman with a coke habit from hell and a lust for kinky sex.

She blames Berlin completely with its anything goes in this city of sin attitude. Nothing like her days back in Sydney.

She remembers the first time she'd gone to the Kit Kat Klub in Kruetzberg and was blown away by what she saw.

To be let in, you must be wearing something sexy and revealing. The more flesh you are exposing, the more chance you have of getting in.

As Jodie tried to get served by one of the many beautiful and naked bar staff she watched, mesmerised, as a woman lay across the bar, legs spread wide, while another equally hot woman licked her pussy.

It was a shock, and she didn't know where to look at first, but after realising they didn't care who was watching, she carried on. And got very horny indeed.

The night just got better by the minute. She then discovered the swing.

Anyone is free to jump on it and swing themselves out into the crowd giving whoever is in its path a chance to either fuck you, lick you or finger you. Whatever takes your fancy.

She finds a spot behind the swing and watches the crowd and the people and all the sex that is going on around her.

The funniest part of her night is watching a man dressed in leather, sitting close to the dance floor on a chair, wanking himself silly to all the sex going on around him. He eventually cums in his hand, eats it all and then falls asleep. Sometime later, he will wake up and repeat the process. Gross and funny all at the same time.

Jodie's non-participation didn't last long. On her third visit, she'd tried out the swing and by the fifth visit, she was known as Madame Piss and could often be found in either the men's or women's toilets pissing on someone who'd begged for it.

Johaan, her German lover and business partner, has no idea about her other life, and she does not care. He is married, though separated and only keeps her as his plaything when he gets the chance.

Jodie has a chuckle to herself remembering her first time in Kit Kat, and she's now keen to get back to Berlin and resume her crazy life after three equally crazy days with William.

William is the biggest party animal she knows, and together they are lethal.

As she sits on her flight, waiting to take off from Heathrow on the last flight out of London, she contemplates ordering a whiskey to kill the sickness, and then she spots Fur Coat.

Long blond hair, legs up to her armpits and dripping with gold jewellery and wearing a huge fur coat that touches the ground. She silently prays Fur Coat is not seated next to her, but after a quick glance around and realising the flight is almost empty, she guesses that Fur Coat could not possibly be seated next to her.

Jodie is wrong, and Fur Coat dumps her bag in the middle seat along with her fur coat and makes herself comfortable on the aisle seat.

Fuck sake, thinks Jodie and buries her head in a magazine to shut down any conversation. But to her dismay, Fur Coat starts talking.

'You don't mind da?' as Fur Coat points to her stuff, taking over the middle seat.

Jodie guesses she must be Russian or Eastern European and nods her approval, hoping that's the last of the conversation and she can get back to reading her boring British Airways Mag.

No such luck.

'Fuck it so hot, but my coat too big for locker da?' Fur Coat loudly sniffs throughout her one-sided conversation.

'We need drink, da? I order for us' sniff.

Reluctantly Jodie puts down her magazine. Having established Fur Coat isn't going to shut up and estimates 1.5 hours of making small talk isn't that torturous.

As soon as the flight takes off, Fur Coat has the Steward waiting on them hand and foot as if she's the Queen and making the flight way more enjoyable than Jodie had been expecting.

'Hey, you keep sniffing like a coke head; what's that all about?' says Jodie hopefully. She recognises it instantly and thinks fuck it, let's end my London trip on a high. Which she does.

It turns out that Fur Coat is a high-class Escort on her way to see a client for the weekend, and she's carrying 10 grams of coke and 5 grams of powdered heroin.

'It's for pain, to help me with pain,' says Fur Coat to a slightly confused Jodie.

'What pain?'

'For the pain he will put me through, I will get £1000 a night,' she says with a sad wink.

Up until that moment, Jodie had been harbouring a glamourous thought about what it would be like to fly around the world meeting clients for sex. Not anymore.

Fur Coat gives Jodie a gram and a rolled-up £50 and insists she go have herself a line or two and Jodie doesn't need to be told twice.

In the cramped toilet, Jodie manages to cut up two rather fat lines of some of the purest cocaine she has ever had, and her nose explodes with blood all over the place.

While she's cleaning herself up, there is a knock at the door, and Jodie panics. It's the Steward, and she's been busted. She opens the door and its Fur Coat wanting to join her for a cheeky line.

She squeezes herself into the tight space and starts to kiss Jodie deeply and slowly until it becomes frantic and horny.

'I'm horny, touch me please,' begs Fur Coat, but Jodie draws the line at going near her pussy. It's bad enough that she has her tongue in her mouth where God only knows what's been in it.

Fur Coat senses her reluctance and starts to pull Jodie's jeans and knickers off. She gets down on her knees, all the while touching herself under her dress and gives Jodie the best oral sex she has ever had. It isn't long before both girls have an orgasm.

Panting and flushed, they both get dressed and try to discreetly leave the toilet and return to their seat.

As they go to sit down, the male Steward gives them a knowing smile and a wink of approval.

Jodie can honestly say it's the best flight she's ever taken.

13

'Look, William, I haven't called in sick for ages. You know I must be ill to call on a Monday' I croak down the phone to Willy who has just received a call from me late on this Monday morning.

'Even if I were hooked up to a drip, I'd still come to work Bree' says Willy unhelpfully.

'As I said before, I'm feeling pretty rough. I've been up all night with something bad and I need to get back to bed.' I'm already in bed and the bad thing I've been up all night with is prodding his throbbing cock into my back, expecting to find my hole.

'Well, you sound hungover, but as I can't see you, I just have to take your word for it Bree. Just make sure you get some rest and you're in tomorrow ok' and with that William hangs up which means I can go back to doing Mr Bad.

So, how did I end up in Mr Bad's bed, somewhere in Dollis Hill North West London, well I met him at Church yesterday. No, not The Church but *The Church*. London's craziest Sunday session ever. Now Jess and I had heard about the Church from almost every Australian or Kiwi we had ever met, but we've never been invited or had the desire to shlep out at 11am on a Sunday morning and get to Kings Cross where it is currently situated. I wished I'd discovered this place beforehand; it was wild.

Jess and I decided on a whim to make the journey to Kings Cross as we'd had a quiet Saturday night and we were both bored and ready to party and Jess also thought it might be a good way for me to get my mind off Juan. When we'd got to the Cross it wasn't hard to find the Church, we just followed the huge crowds of backpackers, carrying cans of lager in their carrier bags, heading towards their Sunday session. Whilst waiting in the queue, which snaked around the venue, we were helpfully informed that under no uncertain terms should we tell the bouncers that we are English. Apparently, Pom's are banned from entering, according to the lovely Australian girls who had taken us under their wing.

'Yeah nah mate, don't tell them yous are whinging poms, they won't let ya in' said one of them.

'Where shall we say we're from?' asked Jessie quite concerned. We didn't fancy standing around for an hour, only to be told to 'fuck off, no poms.'

'Dunno mate, probably some ass end place in Oz or NZ' she continued.

'How bout Dubbo, or Timaru,' said the other helpful Antipodean.

When it came to our turn to get in the bouncers stop us, they can smell Pom a mile away and I honestly believed we were about to be turned away, but Jess put on her best Aussie/Kiwi accent, confirming we are in fact from Timaru, and we were ushered in. It took a few seconds for the sights and sound to hit us but fuck me, what a place. Sawdust covering the floor and thousands of people dancing, drinking, snogging, and singing to 80's Antipodean rock. The place was rocking. The queue to get drinks was a nightmare and we understood why everyone who eventually got to the bar ordered all their drinks for the day, not caring much that they had to drink them warm.

We did the same. Six cans of cider each and we made our way to the middle, squeezing through the crowds, getting our tits and arses rubbed and pinched by random men as we pushed passed them, a small price to pay to get into the middle of it all.

We found a spot, tied our carrier bag of cans to our jeans and danced. Throughout the day various entertainment came and went on stage including competitions to win beer. Get your tits out for the boys, win a 6 pack. Get naked for the boys, win multiple 6 packs, and then Dick Dastardly the male stripper came on and the crowd of girls went wild and we happily joined in. We all wanted to be smacked around the face by his cock. He was flinging that thing against any face that could get to the front of the stage and I managed to elbow my way to the front and get a slap. It was almost the highlight of my day. Jess later confessed she wished she'd been smacked in the face by DD.

The amount of drink we consumed in such a relatively short time was impressive and to say we were drunk towards the end of the day, was an understatement and then I saw Mr Bad. Tall, long almost mullet styled hair, no shirt on and quite a skinny body, but the eyes told me a different story. He had been watching me dance and we had locked eyes several times and smiled goofily at each other. It didn't take long for Jess and me to find ourselves dancing in his circle of friends and we wasted no time and started pashing within seconds. I spent the rest of the afternoon stuck to his face and Jess was doing the same with someone else from the circle. At one stage I must have looked around and realised most of The Church were snogging.

We were invited to The Backpackers which is just around the corner and we left with the circle. What was surprising was leaving The Church at 4pm and stepping out into bright daylight. Being inside the Church, you felt like you were in a nightclub, in the middle of the night, not the day, and stepping out onto the streets of London, with sober, normal people was probably the oddest thing about the day. We didn't complain though, we continued into the night at another crazy Antipodean pub.

It was a guarantee I was going home with Mr Bad and another bonus came my way when we got back to his flat and he had a gram of coke and a bottle of Jack Daniels just waiting there for us, as if he knew he was going to pull an all-nighter.

Mr Bad finds his hole and starts fucking me from behind. As I look out into his room, I spot my jeans lying on his floor, covered in sawdust, and still dripping in cider and beer from the day before and I groan, not just in pleasure but at the thought of having to put them back on and get back to my house in Chiswick. But right now isn't the time to think about that, Mr Bad is good, and he wants to fuck me again, I don't complain. He's from New Zealand, has a massive cock and has been fucking me most of the night.

When I told Willy I was too ill to come into work, I wasn't lying, I'm hanging from the drugs and drink I consumed yesterday but I wouldn't change a thing.

After what seems like hours Mr Bad and I finally finish our morning session and decide we need to smoke and drink a coffee and he goes to make me one. While he's in the kitchen I reluctantly get dressed in my minging jeans but getting them back on is so painful as they are still soaking wet and stink of beer.

Mr Bad comes back with my coffee and a spliff but I'm eager to leave and get home. It's been fun but I don't want to overstay. I'm not interested in seeing him again. One night is more than enough.

'Thanks for a great night' I say as I go to leave.

'Hey, I don't even know your name' says Mr Bad.

'A bit late for that' I laugh.

'Thanks gorgeous, I won't forget ya in a hurry that's for sure.'

And with that I shlep back to Chiswick, covered in sawdust and stinking like a brewery, looking like a cheap whore doing the walk of shame, but not caring one bit at the odd looks I get on the Tube.

14

They've been engaged for several weeks now and how is my plan on winning him back going? Well, pretty shit, really.

I'd planned to get thinner, and yet after a month of being on the C Plan (coke, coffee and ciggies), I remain 53kgs. Fuck. The extra money I wanted to earn in order to propel myself into riches beyond my wildest dreams, fell flat on its face before it even begun.

I'd bought an ounce of cocaine (costing a small fortune I might add, even though I'd got it at wholesale price), and if I'd sold at the right price, I'd have ended up with a healthy profit.

The only problem with this arrangement is my love of coke and I have snorted most of it (refer to C Plan), and the 4 grams I have sold are all on tick, and I am yet to see a penny of the money. Bugger.

And since that night in the Redback, I have only heard from Juan once and that was after I'd sent him a text asking if he'd like to catch up sometime. He'd responded with a promising yes, with which I responded 'when?' and I'm still waiting for the reply.

So you see, my plan to win him back isn't going so well, and I'm miserable as hell but will not give up as I need this man back in my life. Why? Well, that's a question I ask myself daily.

I think everyone's patience is running out with me when it comes to my quest to get him back, so I keep quiet most of the time.

At least Spring is only around the corner. This winter has been long and dark and I'm over it. It also means that we are one season closer to them getting married. My stomach does a flip at the thought of Juan and Bitchface getting married. But I have a plan. I'm going to win him back, and I'll be the one walking down the aisle with him, not her.

I stop daydreaming and continue to clean the house. Jess has rented out the box room at the top of the stairs to Surfer Boy from J-Bay. Apparently, he is hot, and I've strict instructions not to shag him. As if!

I've stocked the fridge with Castle Lager and picked up some Biltong. I've also been smoking weed all day as I'm sure he'll love to walk into a house that smells like Amsterdam. I want to make a good first impression.

Surfer Boy doesn't disappoint. Long blond-hair, blue-eyes, tanned and a body to die for. It's going to be hard not to shag this man and I start acting like a stupid teenager.

'Would you like a beer? Spliff?' I overdo it and make things awkward and make him feel uncomfortable, and this is all before he's even seen his room.

He's a friend of Pablo, so I know he must love the stuff.

Jess shows him around and leaves him in his room to unpack and invites him down to the lounge for a drink and smoke when he's finished.

When he eventually comes down, he's only keen for a beer but doesn't share the joint with us.

I'm excited that our boring Saturday night might turn into something fun. It doesn't.

He says he's too tired and needs an early night due to his plans for Sunday and goes to bed. We both feel slightly disappointed.

We don't see him Sunday and by the time Monday rolls back around, we've seen our new hot flatmate for precisely 2 hours this weekend.

He really isn't turning into the flatmate I'd hoped!

I find myself walking to work again on another Monday but today feels slightly different.

I stop my thoughts of Juan and try and work out why this Monday doesn't suck as much as usual. I notice the trees first. They are slowly coming back to life after a long cold winter. Not by much, just the odd green leaf that has appeared, but enough to know that Spring is finally on its way.

And something else too, and I can't quite put my finger on it, and just as I'm about to push the thought away, I remember.

I didn't cry this morning in the shower like I usually do over Juan. Does this mean I'm finally over him? I think of the wedding planning he and Bitchface must be doing, and the rage and jealousy come flooding back. Phew! I'm not over him; I'm just learning to live with it. I am relieved.

I also have a plan and a new flatmate. Life could be worse. For the first time in weeks I walk through the doors of Man Source on a Monday with a smile on my face.

'Fuck me, someone got lucky,' says William when he sees me.

'For your information Willy, I did no such thing' and I make my way to my desk. I'm happy to get started with work. I do, however, need a cigarette and hope that William will want all the gossip in the courtyard.

'Well, it certainly beats the face of a mourning widower with bee sting eyes that we've all been subjected to these last few weeks' continues William.

Fuck he can be a bitch, but he does have a point.

'So, what's his name?' asks Jonny, who's also made it to work on time. Now I'm suspicious and look around the office expecting to see The Pikey.

She has not arrived on a surprise visit. Thank fuck. No, it's just the stars have aligned for everyone today; trains were on time, and hangovers were minimal.

'I have a new flatmate and he is delicious, and I think I'm going to sleep with him,' I tell the crew.

'Ah, I knew it had to be man related,' quips Willy from his desk.

'Ver he from?' asks Aggie.

'South Africa, and he's a surfer,' I say proudly.

Aggie looks unimpressed and goes back to doing nothing at her desk.

'Get a photo of him; I want to see how good looking this surfer is,' says William.

'I don't have a photo, William, and where on earth would I get one. Just believe me when I say he's pretty damn hot.'

William doesn't believe me and goes back to work.

I vow to get a photo of Surfer Boy and prove just how hot my next shag is.

I start this Monday on a high, an absolute high, and I like it.

15

As I walk home, trying to work out whether I've had a good day or not, a thought strikes me. We need a party.

Jess and I haven't had one in ages, not a proper party where loads of people come over and stand around, squashed into the lounge and kitchen. Where drugs are openly taken and booze flows freely.

I will suggest it to Jess when she gets home later tonight, but Jess doesn't like throwing parties at the house due to the massive clean up the next day. She's also scared the house will get trashed, and she has a right to feel this.

The first party we ever threw after I moved in, nearly ended in disaster when a travelling mob of gate crashers tried to get in. When they were refused entry, they proceeded to vandalise several parked cars on the street. The neighbours were furious, and we spent an hour talking to the cops the following morning, after they had turned up to investigate.

I will need a good reason to have one and Surfer Boy is it. We need to show our new flatmate just how cool and wild we are, and I want to show off to my friends just how gorgeous he is.

But first I need to somehow find a photo of Surfer Boy so that I can bring it to work and show my doubting work colleagues that I'm not exaggerating on his good looks.

I hatch a plan on my way home. Yet another plan. My life is full of plans. My life is one big plan!

I get home before any of my flatmates and seize the opportunity to go into Surfer Boy's room on the way to my own, as his door is slightly open, and I can see his rucksack and all its contents strewn across the floor.

I flick through his stuff, and bingo! I find a pack of photos and proceed to ever so quickly go through them. And then I see it, the perfect photo. I make sure all his stuff is put back where he'd left it and I dash to my room for a closer inspection of my prize photo.

I lie on my bed and look longingly at the photo. Surfer Boy is dressed in board shorts and nothing else. His muscly and tanned body is on display, with his hand on his hips. He's semi smiling at someone who is taking the photo and his long blond hair is untied, wet and falling down his back and over his shoulders. It's a perfect photo and I'm ready to fuck him right now. But I can't because he's not here and I have stolen his photo.

I'm about to sort myself out when I hear someone moving around in the kitchen. Someone is home. I park the horny thoughts of Surfer Boy, roll a joint, and make my way downstairs to see who it is.

Surfer Boy and Jess are both home at the same time and they are trying to get some dinner cooked so that they can eat and go to bed. The worst day of the week is over.

Jess and I have Sainsbury's own lasagne and salad, and Surfer Boy has steak and veggies. We eat without saying too much and we watch the Simpsons while we get stoned. It's a good, easy night.

By 9pm we are ready for our beds and wish each other a good night and depart to our respective rooms. A few minutes later, as I'm getting ready to jump into bed, Surfer Boy knocks quietly on my door, and when I open it, my stomach does a flip with concern. He doesn't look happy. I check to make sure the photo is not on my bedside cabernet but in the top drawer where I've hidden it.

'Hey Bree, I'm missing a photo from my collection; I don't suppose you've seen it?' he asks suspiciously. Fuck.

'Um, a photo, what type of photo?' I stammer, trying desperately hard to sound like I am not guilty.

'One of me from my trip to Mexico. My ex took it and it sort of means a lot.' He now sounds sad. Ah crap.

'Um, no mate, but I'll be sure to look out for it. Um, by the way, we are having a party Saturday night, bring your friends,' I say, trying to change the subject and not caring that I haven't run anything past Jess yet.

'Yeah, sure,' he says distractedly and then moves onto Jess's room to ask her about the photo.

After Jess has sworn blind, she hasn't seen the missing photo, she comes to see me.

'So, where's the photo and what fucking party?' she's semi smiling as she says this. I bring it out so that we can both lust over it.

'I can't believe you took it, Bree,' whispers Jess 'how are you going to get it back?'

'I'm not sure, but I'm also really fucking surprised at how quickly he found out it was missing. He's either got a very good memory or he's very vain and just loves that photo.'

We both nod and agree to my last statement.

'So, we are having a party, are we?' says Jess, not very excitedly.

'Yeah babe, sorry I had to say something to get his mind off the photo.'

'You'll be doing the cleaning then?' says Jess.

'Sure will,' but Jess knows I won't.

I'm happy. We have a party this Saturday and I have a Surfer Boy photo; I can show the team.

He is lush, and I plan to fuck him this weekend.

As if Jess can read my mind, she says, 'don't fuck him Saturday; it will end in tears.'

'I sure won't, Jess.'

We both start laughing at this because she knows I will, God willing.

16

Three sleeps until the party and I have barely thought of Juan and Bitchface and their impending marriage.

I reflect once again on my plan and consider whether I've made any leeway.

I haven't.

I still weigh the same today as I did at the start of the plan despite my best efforts. I'm not rich in any way, shape or form. In fact, I'm probably a lot poorer now than when I first started, due to my diet plan.

Has Juan tried to contact me or give me any indication of his desire to be with me? The answer is no. Do I care? A little.

However, I've had a thought. I'm going to invite Juan to the party. Call me crazy, but it is a good reason to reach out and contact him. I first want to run it past the team to see what their thoughts are, but right now, it's just Aggie and me in the office, and it's gone 9am.

William and Jonny have gone back to being late most days and the early mornings are being left to Aggie and myself.

'You have lots of vimen come Saturday, ya?' enquires Aggie.

She's awful at small talk and I'm not in the mood for it today. I want to show off Surfer Boy's photo, and I'm annoyed the boys are late.

'Don't worry, Aggie, I've ordered plenty of pussy for you babe,' I lie.

There's a reason we call her Aggie the Slaggie. She really does seem to fuck a different girl every week.

It's 9.45am, and the boys are still not here, so I go into the courtyard to die. Two cigarettes later, William comes rushing out to join me, ciggie already lit and a coffee in the other hand.

'The fucking traffic, I swear it's getting worse,' he moans. 'I can't leave my flat any earlier than I do, I swear, Bree.' He continues.

I give him a look that says, 'really?'

He lives in Shepherds Bush and literally must only drive down one road, The Uxbridge Road, and if he left earlier than his usual 8.45am, he'd make it on time.

'So darl, how was your night?' asks Willy, but before I can inform him of the photo stealing activities of the night, William proceeds to tell me all about his fabulous night at the Old Compton pub. It sounds like a wild night, and not for the first time. I'm surprised at just how much fun gays can have on a casual Monday night in London.

'I got the photo,' I eventually get to say.

'Fabulous darl, let's go in and see.'

And with that, we finish smoking and rush back to the office to lust after my flatmate.

Jonny is now in, too, so we all gather around my desk and have a good look at the photo of my scrummy, soon to be fucked, flatmate.

'Are you sure he's not gay?' asks Willy hopefully.

'I wouldn't be surprised,' says Jonny.

'Only one way to find out boys, and I intend to do that Saturday night.'

We go back to work as it's now 10.30am, and not much has been done by any of us. Nothing new then.

The day seems to be dragging, and all I can do is dream about Surfer Boy and Juan and planning the party.

'I think I want to invite Juan,' I say to the team, who are all pretending to be busy.

'What? No darl, I really think that's a bad idea,' William is the first to sound horrified.

'Um, I thought you wanted to fuck Surfer Boy?' says Jonny, which is true.

'Das ist nicht so gut' contributes Aggie.

But I'm not looking for permission, and anyway, I've already typed up the text. I just need the courage to press send.

'Hey Juan, we're having a party Sat night. You're invited. No fiancés allowed!'

I laugh at how funny I am.

I go over and read it to Aggie for some girlie feedback and advice. She only repeats what she has said before. It's a bad idea, Bree, blah, blah blah.

I move on to Jonny. He'll give me better feedback.

'Jonny, read this please babe, and tell me what you think.'

He reads it and seems impressed.

'Bree, you're gonna send it whatever I say, so just do it, but be prepared for rejection, my friend.'

He looks concerned for me. I'm just pissed off I even asked him.

I find Willy in the courtyard dying; I spark up a Marlboro and show him the message.

'Bree, you are setting yourself up for misery, but hey, you never listen to me.'

He's right, and I press send. Now I must wait, which I hadn't thought of 5 seconds ago. Fuck.

It has now been 4 hours since I sent the text and still nothing—the bastard. Everyone is right, and I am wrong. What did I really expect from a man who dumped me to get married to Bitchface? He's not coming to the party and I feel low and a little bit stupid. I then remember I still might have a chance with Surfer Boy and my day doesn't feel as dark.

As I sit at my desk going through the database, the front door opens and in walks Two pence lady. She's a local nutter who occasionally pops in and throws Two pence pieces at us whilst cackling with laughter.

She does it today, but this time she hits Aggie straight in the face and draws blood. Aggie is raging and it takes myself and Jonny to hold her back as she leaps towards the nut job. She's ready to punch the crazy bitch out.

William ushers crazy bitch out onto the street and threatens to call the police if she ever does it again.

'If I ever see that voman again, I vill slit her throat,' growls Aggie. Not one of us doubts her for a minute.

17

I intend to give out the E's for free as a 'welcome to our party' gift. This should get things started and Jess agrees this is a good idea.

We have spent the day cleaning the house, to Oasis of course, and getting it ready for tonight, sorting out the alcohol and soft drink needed. The afternoon has been spent slowly getting ready for what we hope is an epic party.

I warm a plate up in the microwave for a few seconds, pour out a generous amount of coke, chop up four healthy lines and bring it upstairs where Jess and Surfer Boy are getting ready in their rooms.

Tonight is going to be fabulous!

I have dirty blond hair, mud brown eyes, I fit comfortably into a size 10/12 jeans depending on which shop I buy from, and my tits are like pancakes with a strawberry on top. Tonight, however, I have sun-kissed bleached blond hair that looks bouncy, as if I've just walked out of a hair salon; my eyes are a sparkling hazel colour with a tint of green. I'm a size 8 with a washboard stomach, jeans falling off my hips and perfectly formed double D tits with erect nipples pointing towards the sky. Have I had plastic surgery and a visit to the salon? No. I've had two lines of some of the purest coke in town and I'm looking fabulous darling!

Jess and I finish off getting ready, confirming what we both already know. We are Supermodels, and we will be the best-looking girls at the party. The mirror does not lie, my friend.

I'm just finishing off my lip gloss when Surfer Boy comes into my room. Jess has already finished and gone downstairs to greet the first guests. My stomach flips with excitement. Surfer Boy is looking at me as if it's the first time he's met me.

'Hey Bree, fuck, you look good' I know this. I smile my 'come get this' smile, and he comes over to me, puts his beautiful brown and muscly arms around my waist, feels my bare skin (washboard) and kisses me lightly on the lips.

The shock of electricity courses through my body, erecting my nipples and clit and sends me into overdrive. I go in for some more, but he pulls away and laughs. 'Later, beautiful,' and walks out smiling. I'm ecstatic and know tonight it is going to happen. I just hope Juan doesn't turn up now. I'm shocked that I think like this already, but happy I might be moving on at last.

'Oh my god, these pills are awesome,' Jonny is coming up from the drugs as a group of us are sitting around in the garden listening to the music and watching as people come and go. The party is in full swing, and because I'm so off my face, I'm not really mingling inside with everyone. I know Jess will be hosting as it's her house, and she knows I'm shit at that when I'm on the drugs. I prefer to be with my small group of friends out in the garden where it's not so hot and claustrophobic.

Jonny and William turned up together and were given a pill as they walked through the door. They didn't ask any questions, just accepted the pill and the bottle of water to wash it down with and carried on past me to the kitchen to drink. Aggie is yet to turn up.

'So what's going to happen if Juan turns up Bree?' William asks, quite concerned after hearing about me and Surfer Boy. 'I have no idea, Willy,' I admit. 'I'm sure I'll be excited to see him, but I don't think he'll come. Bitchface won't let him.'

'You could do both,' winks Jonny and he's right, I can do both. An option I hadn't thought of until now. I can feel my pill seeping into my blood, and I know at any moment I am going to get another drug rush and the world will be a dancing frenzy of love.

The music from the lounge is pulsing and people are dancing and laughing and, by the looks of it, having a brilliant time.

The rush I'm feeling is overpowering, and I make my way upstairs to my room. I need a bit of space away from the crowd and I also fancy another line. I check myself in the mirror and bend over the side table to snort the line I had already prepared earlier, and Surfer Boy comes up behind me and grabs my arse. I knew he'd follow me.

'Hey gorgeous, how's your night going? I just wanted to check you are ok.' Before I can answer, we are snogging like a pair of teenagers, he feels good and tingly against my face. He pushes me passionately towards my bed, and I'm tempted to just go with it, but it's way too early to start that right now. I'm keen, but I can wait.

'Woo, wait up babe, I want this as much as you, but I want to party first, have a line with me' His obvious hard-on and face look disappointed, but I reassure him this is a sure thing and we will fuck tonight. That's if Juan does not show up, but only I know this.

'Let's go party before we come back to play,' I indicate to my bed. 'Ok Bree, but it's a date, ok? I want you on my cock and soon!' A wave of pure horn sweeps through my body. 'Yeah, I need it too.'

As I walk down the stairs, I can see the party is in full swing, and I join the team on the makeshift dance floor, aka lounge/diner and start my awesome dancing. I'm gorgeous, I'm fabulous and if I'm not mistaken, the best dancer here.

'Thanks for invite, you have nice house' Aggie had arrived at some stage while I was upstairs and has dropped her pill. It still hasn't helped with her abysmal small talk; however, as I'm racing off my face and love the world, I attempt to talk to her too. It does not last long, and I wander off to the kitchen to see where Surfer Boy and his mates have gone.

I find them in the garden and I go over to him, put my arm around his neck and start kissing him deeply. I do not care he is mid-sentence and I do not care that his friends are taking the piss out of us. I just want him.

'Hey Bree, how you doing babe, are you having fun?' It's Jess looking loved up and happy. She's not stressing about the mess, which is a good thing. 'I'm awesome gorgeous girl, just like you,' and we hug and cuddle and start dancing on the spot. Surfer Boy has other ideas and starts pulling me away and towards the stairs trying to get me back to the bedroom and this time I can't resist. I give Jess a knowing wink and leave the party behind to go shag this beautiful man.

As I walk out of the garden and into the house, I notice Aggie chatting up a hot brunette. I have a chuckle to myself because, despite Aggie's shit social skills, she always lands a pussy for the night.

We forget foreplay and go straight for penetration; we are both too horny to worry about the other stuff. He pulls my jeans down, doesn't wait for me to take them off and takes me from behind, and I'm so wet he finds my pussy easily and slips his throbbing cock into me and starts fucking me hard. My jeans are wrapped around my ankles, making it hard to spread my legs, but I think he likes this because it's feeling a lot tighter down there. I know he isn't going to last long, but I'm ok with that. I don't want to spend the whole night in bed. That can wait until the party has started to die down.

I'm right, Surfer Boy cums in less than a minute, and I can tell by his groans that he needed it more than I did. 'Babe fuck, that was good and quick, sorry,' he says, quite embarrassed. 'Hey, all good, it was great, you can finish me off later,' and he nods with a grin.

We are not ready to go downstairs just yet, and we both lie on the bed, giggling and talking and basking in the one minute of glorious sex. I have a half-smoked joint in the ashtray next to my bed and I reach over and light it up. We both sit back and smoke in silence and listen to the music pumping through the floor below.

'I've been wanting to do that to you since I met you,' he says.
'Me too,' I reply.

I need to use the toilet, so I indicate for him to get my coke out of the drawer and cut up a couple of lines ready for my return.

I pull my jeans and knickers back on and head downstairs to make my way through the party and into the toilet, trying not to talk to anyone as I'm keen to get back. I clean myself off and head back upstairs in anticipation for one more shag and a few lines before joining everyone again.

As I walk into my room, I can tell something has changed just by looking at his face, and then I see it in his hand. The photo I had stolen just the other day and that I'd forgotten was in my top drawer.

'What the fucks this, Bree?' Surfer Boy says accusingly. At first, I don't really see the seriousness of it all. We'd just had a great one minute shag and we have coke to snort.

'Ah, that old thing, don't worry about that right now; you have more important things to worry about,' I say as I start to undress, hoping to deflect him from the issue at hand. But he's having none of it and he looks really pissed off.

'You fucking lied to me and went through my stuff, mate' I'm beginning to feel really uncomfortable and unhappy with how this conversation is going. Even my tits hanging out don't seem to be doing anything to calm him down.

'I can't fucking trust you, man; you're just another snake with tits,' and he goes to walk out.

'What the fuck, don't take it so seriously, come back to bed and fuck me again,' I plead; I'm horny and I'm getting annoyed that he has had his fun and now he wants to bail out.

'Fuck you Bree, that isn't happening,' and off he walks.

I'm flabbergasted and then I start to cry because I don't know what else to do. I'm feeling embarrassed and used and so disappointed. Now I don't want to go downstairs. I get dressed and sit in my room for a while, snorting coke and smoking spliff until I know Jess will come find me.

'What's happened Bree? Surfer Boy and his mates just left, he looked so pissed off.'

I start to tell Jess what happened but can't stop crying, and she's mortified I'm wasting our perfect party over a photo. After 20 minutes of feeling sorry for myself, I eventually go downstairs to carry on, but the glow in me has gone, and I proceed to get absolutely hammered.

As I fall asleep alone, sometime before 5am, I know I will wake up with the dreaded cringe factor, but right now I don't care. I just want this night to be over and sleep to take me.

18

So, it is official, Surfer Boy has moved out. Apparently, he cannot live with someone he can't trust. Dick. But he had a good one, and he knew how to use it, even if it was only for a minute. I had cringe factor yesterday morning when I had woken up in my hungover state, but today, I am a little bit raging. Personally, I think it is a huge overreaction. It is not like I stole money or drugs. It was a photo!

And to top it all off, Juan had turned up sometime in the night when I was upstairs with Surfer Boy and had promptly left when he found out I was upstairs and busy. So, it's a double whammy for me right now and I'm all fucked up and torn between wondering why Juan came to see me and did he want to get back together and Surfer Boy leaving me high and dry.

Apart from the photo fuck up and a missed opportunity with Juan, the party was a good one. In fact, I believe it was our best so far, and the team agree with me.

Another one bites the dust, and if I am honest, I am gutted. I cannot even hold down a shag for longer than a night, and I had no intention of making him a one-night stand as I liked him. I need to get over Juan, and I thought he would be the one to do it. I was wrong.

The team want to gossip about the weekend, and I don't. I am still ropey from the weekend, and I am feeling sorry for myself.

'So darl, want to talk about Saturday night?' asks Willy as he gestures towards the courtyard, implying we should go outside and smoke.

I have not been outside for a smoke since arriving at work an hour ago, and he is looking concerned. Maybe he thinks I am going to have an emotional outburst.

'No Willy, I'm trying to cut down.'

With that, the team start laughing at my ludicrous statement, and the spell is broken. I smile for the first time that day.

'Come my china, spill the beans; we want all the details of Saturday night,' pleads Jonny.

Fuck it, they will know eventually, so I spend the next twenty minutes spilling the beans about Surfer Boy finding the photo and leaving me naked and gagging for him. I also tell them he has already moved out and that Juan had turned up, which I didn't find out about until the next morning.

'Fuck,' mumbles William.

'Ah fuck Bree,' says Jonny.

'Vanker,' says Aggie and then moves back to her desk in disgust.

They are making me feel better by the minute, but I still want Monday over as soon as possible, and I look for things to do to make the day go quickly. No builders are walking through our door this morning and I have a feeling the day is going to drag.

'Welcome to Man Source, In Your Face Recruitment, how can I help you' Willy loves answering the phone and saying the full company title. Aggie, the receptionist, rarely does. She rarely answers the phone when I think about it.

'Oh, hi darl, how are you? Mmm mmm uh-huh, yes it was great, did you have fun?' Willy is nodding along to the other side of the conversation while looking at me.

'Yeah, she is, a bit miserable, but that's to be expected. Yeah, another one bites the dust. Hey, just make sure the next one is a girl,' William is laughing along with Jess, who is obviously on the other end of the call.

I look at William through slitted eyes as he transfers the call.

'It's for you Bree, it's Jess.'

Stating the obvious, you prick.

'Hey.'

'Hey.'

'What's up, Jess,' I really do not feel like another lecture right now after last nights.

We had gone to bed around 5am once the last guests had gone home, and we did not bother to clean the house. We woke to the mess mid-afternoon. Surfer Boy had left with his mates after finding the photo, so it was left to Jess and me to do.

The place was a mess and it took a few lines of coke (surprisingly, I had some leftover) and a couple of spliffs to get our arses into gear to finish the cleaning. We got lucky too. I found a cigarette packet full of weed, and Jess found a bag with 4 pills in it. They were stored safely for another night, though I was tempted to down the lot and go on it again. Jess is the voice of reason, thank God, and convinced me otherwise.

Once the cleaning was completed, we treated ourselves to a feed at The Duke, and after that, we went to Blockbuster and rented Friends to be enjoyed that evening.

As I was about to go to bed, having done a marathon session of Friends, spliff and some left-over wine from the party, Jess was ready for 'the talk'.

'I love you, Bree, you know that right?'

Here we go.

'But don't fuck our flatmate again, ok?'

'Hey, Jess, he isn't pissed off I fucked him; he's pissed off I borrowed his photo; it's no biggie.'

'He's pissed off cos you went in his room, rifled through his rucksack and stole his favourite photo. You showed it to everyone and then denied taking it. He found it after you shagged him!' She did have a point.

'Fair enough, babe, I promise not to take any more of his photos, but I can't promise I'll never shag him again.'

'Bree, he might not be coming back, you know, that right? I don't think you'll be shagging him again' she's probably right.

Surfer Boy had come back in the night and packed up his rucksack and had completely moved out by the time we woke up.

Pussy.

He had left a note for Jess. He had said he would call her later today, hence why Jess was probably calling me at work right now.

'I spoke to Surfer Boy; he's asked for his deposit and week's rent back because he doesn't want to live with a thief' says Jess.

'I hope you said no.'

'He'll get his deposit back but not the rent. Don't fuck the next one.'

'I won't,' I lie.

'I'll see you later. Fancy meeting at the Goldfish bowl for a steak and a wine? I really don't want to cook tonight,' says Jess.

And just like that, I feel happy again. 'Yes, I'd love that. Thank you. See you later, babe, love you.'

19

Aggie had no plans to hook up with anyone because she had recently been used, yet again, by a straight woman looking to try lesbian sex, and she was over it. She loved sex, but she also liked being someone's girlfriend, and it had been a while since she was that. Everyone at work believed otherwise and thought she was a female version of Jonny, but that isn't true. Aggie is lonely and deep down looking for someone to call her own. She did not expect to meet anyone at Bree's party, but she did.

Aggie was off her face quite early on at the party, along with the rest of the team, and she had danced for most of it. It wasn't until later in the evening, when she had been sitting in the garden coming down, that she had started talking to Smokey. Smokey rolled one spliff after the next and chain-smoked the whole time Aggie had been sitting in her circle, and she was impressed. Spliff was exactly what she needed, and Smokey understood this. She was coming down herself and needed to take the edge of the night.

There were a few of them talking, laughing, and smoking. It took a while before Aggie found herself talking directly to her, and she enjoyed their deep conversations about nothing. At the beginning of the conversation, Aggie briefly thought about flirting with her and working out whether she had a chance but gave up on the idea when Smokey mentioned her boyfriend's name quite early on. He was on a boy's night out and hadn't made it to the party. Smokey had ended up partying on her own but didn't seem to mind. She was fun and flirty and had the most amazing green eyes. Aggie had to keep reminding herself not to move in for a kiss on several occasions, and felt she was getting mixed signals from her. It had to be the drugs. Aggie had got it wrong in the past, and she knew it was wishful thinking.

'Where are you from? Your accent is weird,' laughs Smokey. Aggie got this often. A mixture of German, Polish, and most recently London, did make her sound weird. She explained this, and Smokey thought it was cool. 'And you,' inquires Aggie. Smokey informs Aggie she is originally from Israel but has lived in the States for a few years while studying, hence why her accent sounds weird too. The girl's bond over weird accents, and before Smokey leaves for the night to go home, she suggests they meet up for a drink sometime soon when they are both sober. Aggie gives Smokey her number and is disappointed she must leave and forgets all about her until she calls a few days later.

'Hey weird girl, do you remember me?' it's Smokey on the phone and Aggie is surprised to hear from her. 'Of course, how can I forget the spliffs.' Aggie's stomach does a flip.

'I was just wondering if you were free for a drink tonight. There's a lovely wine bar on Chiswick High Street we could meet.' Aggie knew the place well, and even though she did have plans this evening, she was happy to cancel them for a few wines with Smokey. They agree to meet at 7pm that evening which was perfect because it meant she'd be able to get home, have a shower and get ready for the night. Aggie got off the phone and was about to tell the team but stopped herself. She didn't want the piss-taking that she knew she'd get from them about getting another pussy.

Aggie arrived ten minutes early and was surprised to see Smokey sitting at a window seat already, with a bottle of Chardonnay chilling and 2 glasses poured. Again, Aggie had a feeling something else was going on with Smokey but wasn't quite sure.

'You know me already,' says Aggie, indicating her favourite wine, as she sits down opposite Smokey after giving her a brief peck on the cheek. 'I guessed and hoped you liked what I did,' says Smokey with a wink and a smile.

Aggie doesn't quite remember when the atmosphere between them changed, but it happened sometime between the 2nd and 3rd bottle of wine. It was electric. They had been getting to know each other quite intensely, and at one-point, Smokey had leaned in to inform Aggie that her flat wasn't far and would she like to come back for a smoke. Aggie knows what coming back for a smoke means and she hesitates, but only for a second. 'Fuck, why not' thinks Aggie. If this beautiful straight girl wants to try me out, then so be it.

They giggle and laugh all the way to Smokey's flat, which is just off Chiswick High Street and across from the church on the green. It's small, cosy, and decorated tastefully. Aggie is impressed and tells her.

They make their way into the lounge, which is casual and comfortable and Aggie makes herself at home by plonking herself down on the big, squishy sofa that sits opposite the balcony windows. She's offered a drink, but Aggie declines. She now prefers to have a smoke over wine. She doesn't want to get too drunk, only stoned.

And they smoke, talk, and laugh a lot while sharing the joint, and it is Smokey who makes the first move by leaning into Aggie and kissing her gently on the lips. No tongue at first until Aggie reacts, and then their tongues meet. It is a slow, deep, passionate kiss that ends with Smokey sitting straddled over Aggie. Aggie's head is against the back of the sofa with her hands slowly stoking Smokey's back. They are taking things slowly as the passion between them starts to build, and the desire starts to climb. Smokey sits back and takes off her top very slowly to reveal her pert tits, hidden beneath a black lacy bra, and Aggie buries her face between them. Licking her erect nipples through the lace until Smokey undoes it and releases them fully into her mouth. Smokey groans at how good it feels to have her nipples sucked by a warm and gentle mouth, and she knows she isn't going to last long.

Aggie takes her time. She wants to enjoy this moment as she is assuming this is Smokey's first time with a woman, though she can't be sure. She leans her back slightly so that she can snake her tongue along her stomach, and this makes Smokey shudder so suddenly Aggie knows she'll cum as soon as her tongue touches her clit.

She pushes Smokey over to the side and onto the sofa and lies on top of her while kissing her deeply. At the same time, she is reaching for her jeans and undoing them so that she can get them off. When she eventually does, she sees the wet stain that is appearing at the crutch of her matching black knickers, and she bends down to smell her and taste her. Smokey can barely contain her moans as Aggie slowly pushes her tongue up and down her knickers, making sure she touches her hidden clit and working her way back down to where she is soaking wet. She does this for a while until Smokey can't take it any longer. 'Take them off and eat me,' groans Smokey, and Aggie does as she's told. As her tongue enters Smokey deeply, she grabs Aggie's hair and pushes her face deeper into her pussy and starts to grind against her. By the time Aggie makes it to her clit, Smokey is having an orgasm against her face.

Smokey pulls Aggie up from between her legs and kisses her hard and fast, and makes it clear she wants to return the favour, but Aggie tells her to relax, sit back and enjoy the waves of pleasure that are quite obviously still pulsing through her body. She wants a smoke and leans over to spark up the joint that is sitting in the ashtray.

They chat for a while, smoke the joint and laugh at the stories that are being told in their very stoned state. A short time later, Aggies receives the best oral sex she has ever had, and this was from an apparent straight girl. Smokey knows exactly what to do, at the right speed and gentleness that Aggie cries out in pure ecstasy when she climaxes.

The girls continue throughout the night and don't stop until they can hear the birds of London waking up. They both fell asleep in each other's arms and sleep fitfully.

When they wake the next morning, there is no embarrassing silence or the need to leave quickly. They enjoy their morning coffee together, talking about their amazing night, and both decide they aren't quite finished, so jump into the shower and wash each other sensually. They both cum together, each using their fingers and Aggie, at that moment, thinks she could fall in love with this woman.

20

I'm raging, fucking raging, and it's all because of Surfer Boy and Juan. I'm still in disbelief at how Surfer Boy had reacted to 'photogate' and even more upset that Juan had turned up while all the drama had been going on upstairs. If he had stayed for just 10 minutes longer, I would have welcomed him with open arms and forgotten about my cringe factor with Surfer Boy. I had been left a crying mess and alone when I didn't have to be.

The team at work have told me to stop whining about it and leave it be. But I can't. Not for the first time this week do I feel utterly sorry for myself.

I have been tempted to text Juan and ask him to come over, but my pride (yes, I do have some) has stopped me. Also, the team have told me it's a bad idea, as did Jess last night, but still! He came to see me and I wasn't available to him.

I'm trying to do as little as possible today because I need to sit and think about what my next move is going to be. I feel it is momentous that Juan even came to my house after all this time, to do what? Who knows, but he came, and that is the important part of all this. He could have been coming to tell me how much he loved me and regretted leaving me for Charlene. I will never know. Am I dramatic? Of course I'm dramatic!!

I'm about to sneak off to the courtyard to die for the fifteenth time today when the front door of the office opens and in walks eight men all looking for work. I look at them, and they look way too pretty to be construction workers, but they assure Aggie, who is obviously thinking the same that they are, in fact first and second fixers, which in construction talk means carpenters (I only know this shit from working at Man Source).

'Bree, the group need registration ya,' shouts Aggie at me without even looking up from her computer screen. I usher the 2 main men to my desk and ask the others to wait in the reception area. Jonny and Willy have just walked in from dying, and William almost pushes Jonny out of the way to get to the pretty men sitting at the front, offering to help us process their paperwork as we are all quite obviously busy. William only ever offers to help when the men who walk in are hot, gorgeous, or pretty, like the eight currently in my office right now.

They are from Essex and their accent gives them away. Main man one is cute, with perfect skin, white teeth, and manicured nails. I question him again and ask to see his papers. I'm dubious because their hands don't look like they've done a hard day's work in their life.

It takes a couple of hours to process the crew between myself, William and Jonny, and with Willy unashamedly flirting outrageously with a couple of them. They humour him, probably because they think it will guarantee them a start on a site in Berlin, which it does. They are booked in for their 'induction' with Jodie this weekend and they promise to be at Oscar Wildes on Saturday at 12pm sharp.

William calls Jodie later that day to update her on the crew arriving in Berlin that weekend, she is impressed we've managed to find a whole team and one that she needs for her city project.

It's given me a short reprieve from my thoughts and I've welcomed the distraction. I go home that evening in a slightly better mood as my rage subsides.

21

Jonny wanted this girl so badly he thought he would explode if he didn't get her. Scandie blond hair (his favourite), bouncy but firm tits (second favourite) and a beautiful tight arse that was currently being showcased in her jeans.

Jonny is in the Slug & Lettuce at Fulham Broadway having a Saturday afternoon session with his flatmates and he'd spotted Blondie the minute she had walked in with her friends. He was going to take her home later, but first he wanted to drink and take drugs and enjoy being with the boys. It didn't stop him from watching her though. He wanted to make sure nobody else muscled in on his potential shag. She wasn't getting any attention at this stage, but it is early, and the pub is quiet. That would soon change.

They had exchanged a couple of looks throughout the afternoon and eventually they ran into each other as Jonny was on his way to the toilet. He had planned the whole thing and nothing was an accident. He'd been watching her movements and when the time was right, with her on her way to the bar, he had made his move.

As he pushed gently past her, she gave him direct eye contact and smiled. He knew that smile, he'd seen it a million times before. I'm interested in you smile. 'Hey gorgeous, where are you off to?' He knew where she was going, he wanted to make conversation. 'Um just the bar for drinks' her accent was noticeable, and her voice was pure silk. 'May I get it for you?' he indicates to the bar and she says yes, he may.

Jonny proceeds to buy her a vodka and lemonade and starts to make small talk. She doesn't seem in a rush to go back to her friends, as does Jonny, so they stand to the side of the bar and start to chat. He finds out she's from Denmark, lives in Wimbledon and works in the City as a Marketing Executive. Jonny tells her his story. Not all of it as he doesn't want her to know exactly where he lives or works. Not just yet, he needs to work out if she's normal or a crazy bitch. He's learnt the hard way when a psycho bitch from his house share, he had been living at, wouldn't leave him alone after he'd shagged her once. She had assumed they were dating and had tried to move into his room almost immediately and when he rejected her continued advances, she had caused no end of trouble at home, which he eventually had to move out of, but that didn't stop her. She then stalked him at work until his Manager had called the police and had her arrested for throwing a pint of beer over him. Never again will he ever fuck a flatmate or a flatmate's mate.

Jonny and Blondie spend the next 2 hours getting to know each other, flirting, and having a jolly old time. Jonny's friends eventually join Blondie's friends, and it works out well because there is chemistry, and it looks like the whole group are going to get laid. Jonny doesn't care about that. He cares only about taking Blondie back to her place and fucking her. He doesn't have to wait long. They'd been kissing and caressing in the corner of the seating area and not really taking much notice of anyone else. In fact, one of his mates had already left to go to another party and the other one had his tongue down Blondie's friend's throat. This was turning out to be a good Saturday.

'So, are we going back to mine as it's only 6 stops from here?' Blondie didn't have to ask twice. Jonny was pulling her through the crowds of people that had appeared from nowhere, out of the front door and onto the street. As they walk towards the Tube station, they wrap themselves around each other, not caring at the bewildered looks they are receiving and kiss all the way to the platform and onto the waiting carriage of the train. Jonny's hard on is prominent through his jeans and it had been noticed by several passengers, most of whom were just jealous knowing he was about to fuck this beautiful woman. The woman across from them tried to discreetly look at it from time to time and Jonny caught her looking and made her blush. The lovebirds giggle and kiss the whole way back to Wimbledon which is only a 12-minute ride away.

Once they arrive at Wimbledon station, they make the 15-minute journey to her house by foot so that by the time they walk through her front door and into her room they are tearing each other's clothes off and fucking within seconds of getting the door closed. Blondie doesn't even care that her housemates start clapping as she goes up the stairs. She is horny and wants it just as badly as Jonny.

'I need it harder Jonny' is the last words he remembers before the instant wave of unbelievable pain hits him. It is like white lightening hitting his dick and coursing through his body and at first Blondie thinks Jonny is screaming because he has cum. This is not the case. Jonny has just fucked her so hard he has snapped his cock, a penile fracture is the medical term, but Jonny doesn't know that right now. All he knows is he is experiencing the worst pain of his life and he thinks he is going to die from a stroke right at that moment.

'Fuck Jonny what's happening' squeals Blondie when she sees the blood as Jonny collapses beside her screaming and crying like a baby. Jonny can't speak and just lays in a ball holding his dick as the blood pisses out between his fingers. 'Call an ambulance' croaks Jonny between sobs and he writhes around in agony on her bed. Blondie grabs a towel and runs downstairs to the landline phone and calls 999. Her housemates have heard the commotion and have rushed upstairs to see what has happened. A couple of the guys look visibly distressed and shocked and in pain for the poor guy; the girls are just grossed out by the blood.

By the time the ambulance arrives, Jonny is delirious from the pain that has radiated from his groin area and up into his body, and he just wants to get to hospital. He is kept in for 3 days and the surgery for the fracture completed within a few hours of arriving. He spends the next week off work as he can barely walk and needs constant ice packs held against him.

When the team at Man Source are told about Jonny's misfortune, they don't stop laughing for a good half hour and there is speculation he'll never be able to have sex again. Willy is extremely worried for him. The girls think that now, maybe, he'll keep it in his pants for once.

22

So it's happened. The thing I have been praying for, dreaming of and crying over for what feels like years. I got back with Juan last night, and he only left my bed 10 minutes ago, having spent an amazing night doing what we do best. Shagging.

Well, we have not *officially* got back together, we have not had *the* talk yet, but he did say he would call me later today, so I am sure we'll confirm it then.

My thighs are wobbly, and my fanny is throbbing. I am in freshly fucked heaven right now.

I was not going to go out last night after last weekend's massive session, but Jess was restless and wanted to take the pills we had found. I, on the other hand, was quite looking forward to a weekend in front of the telly. So not like me. I am glad she convinced me otherwise.

'Come on Bree, you boring bitch, just a few drinks at The Duke and you don't have to take a pill,' said Jess.

She knows me well and knows there was no way I was going out with 4 pills in my pocket and not taking at least one.

'We can just drop a half?' pleaded Jess.

She was convincing. I said yes, and as I said before, I am so glad I did.

We had got to The Duke at 3pm, and the atmosphere at that time of day was fun and friendly. It was a balmy spring Saturday afternoon and the beer garden was almost full. We ordered our pints of cider and found an empty table tucked in the corner of the garden. A good spot to people watch and grab some much-needed sun. London is a different place when the sun is shining, which is not often. We make the most of it when it does.

We had been downing the pints quite quickly when I spotted Pablo making his rounds. His face is quite famous around these parts, and it looked like he had a few customers in the pub. I wave at him as he makes his way through the garden, and he acknowledges me with a nod which lets me know he will be at our table shortly. Nice one.

'I think we need a gram to top up the pills, Jess,' I declare.

'Really? You want that big a night?' asks Jess, who was the one that wanted a big night!

'Fuck yeah, why not? It's been a week without class A's.' I did have a point. Normally having E's in the house would not last a night with me. I had been sitting on them for 6 days, a first. They were burning a hole in my pocket, but I was also craving the taste of coke.

When Pablo finally makes it to our table, I am two pints down and feeling tipsy. I need a cheeky line to get me through the rest of the night. 'About time, mate,' I remark to him as he sits next to me.

'Sorry babe, you know me, it's my busiest day,' and he gives us both a knowing wink.

I can see a few of the patrons are looking over. They know. They have just bought themselves.

I offer to buy Pablo a drink, and he orders a lemonade. He doesn't drink much when he is working.

When I get back with the drinks, we make small talk and make it look like three mates just catching up. The bar staff also know

Pablo well, they are some of his best customers, and they let him go about his business unchallenged if it isn't obvious.

The Manager is a different story, and if she saw him dealing, she would throw him out of the pub and ban him for life. Not that she is anti-drugs, she just does not want to bring any unwanted attention from the police into her establishment. The bar staff who live above the pub are all partial to drug-taking, and a raid on the place could shut her down.

'So what are your plans tonight babe,' asked Pablo. A stupid question if you ask me as I'd just scored a gram of coke off him.

'A quiet one, I'm sure,' and we all laugh at this. I do not have time to talk; I need to get to the toilet and snort a big fat one up my nose. I make my excuses and head towards the ladies. I leave Jess with Pablo.

I go into the ladies toilets and I am relieved to see there is no one in here as I lock myself into one of the cubicles. I put the toilet lid down, take my gram, bank card, and already to go rolled up note and crouch down and work my magic. I empty enough coke on the lid to make a decent line, and I chop it up as finely as I can until its powder. I stretch the coke into one long line and proceed to sniff it very loudly up both my nostrils. The feeling of awesomeness hits instantly. I remove all evidence of the coke from the lid, make sure all paraphernalia and goods are stored safely in my pocket, leave the cubicle and go over to the mirror. I admire myself for a few seconds. Looking over my face (gorgeous), hair (bouncy, blond and silky), my teeth (celebrity white) and conclude I am probably the prettiest girl in the pub and that everyone will want to sleep with me tonight. Jennifer has arrived at The Duke, and these lucky bastards are going to know it.

I walk over to the table where I had left Jess and Pablo, and I sort of swagger while flicking my hair and smiling at everyone that looks at me. When I get to the table, Pablo's gone and Jess is talking to some randoms that were passing.

She gives me a nod to tell me she is off to the ladies and leaves me talking to the randoms. I've already sussed out that they are way below my league, and I'm not that interested in talking, but I manage to get the topic of conversation around to my favourite subject, me, and spend the next 10 minutes talking non-stop until they get bored and fuck off back to their seats. I am not upset.

Jess returns from the bathroom after 10 minutes, and she is looking rosy-cheeked, bright-eyed and ready to party, which is good because I was feeling the need to move. So now it is time to mingle and be fabulous. I have already spotted a table with a couple of familiar faces, and I let Jess know I am off to talk to them. She has her eye on one of the new barmen that only started last week and is keen to get to know him. She heads towards the main bar inside for a chat and a flirt.

I am interested in one of the guys at the table, he is from Canada, and I have not done a Canadian before. I try to be super fabulous and extra flirty with this one as I fancy a bit of Canadian for my dinner. He seems interested and has asked a few questions that indicate to me that he is interested.

'So, you're English, right?' he asks an obvious question.

'Yes, sorry,' shit, why do I always apologise for being English? We are the best country on earth, right?

'Hey, no need to say sorry, your accent is sublime,' and the way he says that makes me think for sure I am getting laid tonight.

We carry on making small talk until it gets cold and dark and I suggest we move into the bar where I hope Jess is. I didn't have to worry; she'd been sitting at the end of the bar, closest to the hatch where the staff can come in and out and where they all stand around and smoke when not busy.

'Hey girl, I think I've pulled,' I quietly whisper in her ear.

'Ditto,' giggles Jess while looking at New Bar Boy. He is cute, but not as cute as Canada. I wonder who will make it back to the house first. Me I assume because I do not have to wait until closing time.

As I pop to the toilet for yet another round of powdering my nose, Canada offers to get me a drink and indicates where he will be sitting, waiting. I am quite excited that the night is turning out to be fabulous. Who needs Central London when your local pub can produce the goods on any given night?

I check my stash as I cut up another thick line and estimate it should last the rest of the night if I'm careful and don't have to share, though I might just have to if I want to get laid. I remember I have E's as well, so if Canada is up for it, we could always drop them later too. The options were endless and I was a happy girl. And then I walk out of the toilet, and there he is, looking as beautiful as the last time I saw him, and he sees me and smiles. He takes my breath away, quite literally, and I stand there for a few seconds, not knowing what to do. Juan.

'Hey gorgeous, fancy seeing you here' he comes up to me and gives me a light kiss on the cheek and I can smell his aftershave.

He has changed it since I saw him last, and it smells good. He is with a friend I do not recognise, so I do not say hello.

'Juan, wow, what are you doing in this part of town?' I have nothing else, nothing witty, no comeback, no anger. I am simply happy he's here. 'I have a friend over from Spain, and he wanted to see the sights of London and so thought I'd stop in here on our way.' My heart sinks. He is leaving soon. And then I see Canada waving me over to the spot he had been saving and the drink he has bought.

'Um, I have to go, I'm actually here with someone,' as I indicate Canada. Juan does not look around to see who I am pointing to. 'That's ok babe, I'll be over there if you want to join us later,' and he moves off to the back of the pub, saying hi to Jess on his way and finds a seat close to the pool table. Fuck.

Jess gives me a look that says, are you ok and please do not fuck him, but she also sees the look on my face and knows the chances of that happening are zero. I try and make small talk with Canada, but he has somehow lost his shine, and his accent sounds whiney, not sexy. He realises there is a shift in interest as well and seems a bit pissed off that I can't stop staring at the area Juan has moved to, and I'm not really listening to a word he is saying.

'Hey, do you want to save us both a few wasted minutes and just go see your buddy?' I apologise, make my excuses and dart off my chair and over to Juan, who has saved a space next to him, knowing me well enough to know I'd come. I should be mad; I should hit him over the head and throw a pint of cider in his face (all the things I have been dreaming of for the last few months), but I don't. I want to be with him, I want to talk to him, I miss him.

I do not want to talk about Bitchface and Juan doesn't either. He wants to talk to me and find out what I've been up to (shagging every one of Acton's undesirables), how work was (shit, it just pays the bills) and did I currently have a boyfriend (nope, been pining for you, the bastard). Of course, I did not say any of this and made out I had been having a quiet but fun time without him.

Juan is loaded up with coke as he always is and never asks to have any of mine; this means mine will last the night. He buys me drink after drink and he is back to how he used to be; speaking softly in my ear, making me laugh until I nearly wet myself and making me love him and want him all over again. We include his friend throughout the night, but he calls it in at around 11pm and uses the excuse he is up early in the morning going for a bike ride around Hampstead. Juan invites himself back to mine. It was a given really, and it all flowed so naturally.

We snorted coke, had some of the best sex I have ever had, and I mean EVER. This guy went down on me for hours. Bringing me close to orgasm and pulling his tongue away just at the right time. He teased me, fucked me, and made love to me, all the while making me giggle and love life again. When I eventually came, it was earth-shattering, and I think I even screamed at the end. It really was the best session I have ever had with anyone, and we had not even taken an E. He did not want to; he just wanted me, spliff and a few lines. It was perfect.

And now, this morning, as I lie here having just said goodbye to him, I cannot stop smiling. I had mentioned Bitchface briefly before he left, but he shrugged my question off. I will assume this means they are on the verge of breaking up and he is coming back to me.

'I've missed you, Bree,' were his parting words to me. We are getting back together for sure!!

23

William is distracted, and he cannot focus. He has got a lot on his mind, and most of it is to do with work. He has been feeling a vibe from Jodie the last few phone calls, and he cannot put his finger on it. Well, he can; it is because she thinks the Acton office is underperforming and not sending her enough workers.

Jodie has been managing quite well in finding her own workers while in Berlin. All she must do is hang around any of the Irish pubs long enough on any given afternoon and she soon starts talking to men who are desperate for a start on the building sites. When they find out who she is and the name of her company (she is getting quite famous within the construction world of Berlin), they lavish her with alcohol and drugs in the hope she will give them a start. And she usually does.

She has been questioning why she needs the Acton Branch, which is costing her a small fortune in wages and rent. She has a thousand+ workers ready at the click of her fingers in Berlin and she has mentioned this to Willy on several of her calls just lately, hence why he is distracted right now. He is not quite ready to lose this cushy job.

But right now is not the time to be distracted as he looks down on the brown-eyed, blond-haired beauty that has been going to town on his cock for the last 15 minutes. He's lost his erection on several occasions and the poor boy has had to work extra hard to get Willy back to the right kind of stiffness.

Rent Boy, at 23 years old is wishing he had chosen a different career right now on this miserable morning, with his jaw aching and his arse throbbing. He had been 'hired' last night while he was at the Old Compton in Soho. Rent Boy is a familiar face in these parts and Willy knew he was for hire. They had shared a few drinks and a few snorts of coke while flirting outrageously with each other. William had gone to the Old Compton to get laid and paying for it was much easier. Before leaving for the night, Rent Boy quietly reminded Willy of his hourly rate, which did not bother William in the slightest. He had already budgeted for at least 4 hours of fun.

They had caught a cab to William's place in Shepherds Bush, a small one-bedroom garden flat just off the main square and were ripping each other's clothes off the minute the front door had closed. Willy had almost cum in his trousers while in the taxi with all the dirty talk and rubbing that went on. The Black Cab driver was not impressed as he listened in-discreetly throughout the twenty minute journey. He did not stop listening even when Rent Boy got graphic on what he was going to do to William's cock. Black Cab driver figured it was a good way to while away the time, even if some of the conversations did make him feel nauseous.

William had an orgasm within 30 seconds of arriving home. Deep inside the condom that was hitting the back of Rent Boy's mouth. Rent Boy was happy the first round was over and was hoping they could chill for a bit, have a smoke and a few more lines before he had to get back to work. Once they had dressed and sat in the lounge, William set about casting the mood with music, pouring the wine, a plate of white lines and a large spliff ready to be smoked. Rent Boy liked this part of his job, and he intended to sit back and relax for as long as he could.

The relaxing did not last long because Willy wanted to play again. However, by now, Rent Boy was feeling horny and was looking forward to the fun and games that would play out over the next few hours. After finishing their wine and spliff, Willy suggested a shower and Rent Boy was willing as he wanted to make sure his client was clean before doing anything else.

Once back in the bedroom, condoms on them both, they started to fuck. And they fucked hard. William's arse is nice and tight, and Rent Boy had to pull out several times to stop himself from cuming too soon. William had the opposite problem, where he barely touched the sides. William decided not to use this Rent Boy again. Eventually, after a lot of banging, William was able to climax, but Rent Boy was not finished and needed to cum himself. William bent himself over and took it deeply until Rent Boy was finished. All in all, it was a good session and Willy was happy to pay him the £400 that had been agreed.

It was late by the time they were both ready to sleep and William suggested Rent Boy stay over with no extra cost to him and sleep it off. Rent Boy was happy to do this. And now this morning, he was back chowing down on William's cock and wanting to get out of the flat and back home. He needed to pull out all his special moves to get William moving to climax. He worked his magic, cupping his balls and fingering his bum, and within seconds William was done. Thank God. And it was a freebie.

William was happy it was over and Rent Boy was on his way home. He needed to get ready for work and to sort out his team. As he looked out the window onto another raining and miserable

London morning, he swears blind, this time next year, he will be back in Sydney.

24

'We need another flatmate to help with the rent, Bree,' says Jess as we drink coffee before leaving for work. She'd been saying this for a few days since Surfer Boy left, so I knew it was coming, but the thought of having to share our space again, with God knows who isn't appealing this time around. I am still cringing over Surfer Boy and really can't understand the complete overreaction from the idiot. Gorgeous, big cocked idiot.

However, I now have Juan, and I must thank Surfer Boy for that. Juan had turned up at my party quite late, and I had had no idea as I was upstairs with Surfer Boy before it all went tits up. Juan was not impressed when he was told I was 'busy' and had left almost immediately. It wasn't until the next day that Jess had dared tell me. I had been devastated. My shag had turned into a joke, and my Juan had turned up and left. It really hadn't been the best night though lots of people disagreed. According to some, it had been the best party they had ever attended. Free pills will do that.

Juan had been so jealous that I was upstairs shagging (he doesn't know what really happened, and I will not ever tell him) that he realised how much he loved and missed me. Hence the trip to

The Duke to 'find' me. It worked. We are back together, and I could not be happier. Well, I could be happier, he just needs to get Bitchface out of his life for good, something he said he's trying to do, and I'll be the happiest woman in Acton.

'Ok, but make sure he's not hot. In fact, let's have a gay this time,' I suggest hopefully. Jess agrees and places the advert in the TNT Magazine ready for next Monday's edition.

We leave the house together but part ways at the gate. I turn right to join Acton Lane and Jess turns left to go to Chiswick Park Tube. It's a nice late spring Wednesday morning and I'm feeling fabulous about work. Things are ramping up in Berlin and Jodie seems happy with the quality of workmen we are sending over, which is making life in the office stress-free and almost fun.

Though something is going on with Jonny right now. He isn't himself at all. There has been no shagging, no stories of shagging, no lateness due to shagging, and this is so out of character.

'Hey, Jonny, my South African stunner, how are you? How was your weekend?' I ask, hoping he'll tell me he has a new pussy on the go.

'It was ok, didn't do much really, just the usual' and with that, the conversation is over.

'Are you ok, babe? You don't seem yourself?' I ask, concerned.

'What, because I'm not out every weekend screwing chicks, is that it Bree?' says Jonny defensively.

And I'm taken aback at how spiteful and hateful he sounds, so I leave it. Jonny comes over to me a bit later, after realising what a dick he's been and apologises.

'Hey Bree, sorry my china, I didn't mean to bite your head off. I've just got a few things going on that I'm dealing with, ok' he says sweetly.

'What, syphilis?' I ask jokingly, but the joke falls flat and he storms off like a hormonal teenager and I decide I'll leave him be, or we might just end up in an argument.

We've got Sam coming over tonight to see the room, Bree. Make sure you don't smoke before he gets there. He might be a total square who hates dope,' says Jess, who's called me at work. She's had a few calls since the advert came out and Sam sounds promising.

'Well, if he doesn't like dope, is he really going to fit in,' I ask.

'He sounded gayer than Willy, I'm hopeful,' Jess shares. And I'm hopeful. If he's gay, surely, I can't screw it up and shag him.

And he turns out to be just lovely and gay and loves dope and drugs and can move in two weeks. He's hot, but he's gay and both Jess and I are hopeful I won't fuck this one up.

25

So, I've become the other woman and I have no idea how this has happened. Well, I do. That's a lie. I've allowed Juan to continue to fuck me while he is still living with Bitchface. I have threatened to call it off, I've given him the best blowjobs he's EVER had, I've given him sex every time he's come around and I've expected nothing in return except he leaves her and comes back to me. Not much to ask, really.

Jess says I should dump him. Jonny says I should dump him. Willy says I should not even bother calling him and Aggie thinks I don't love myself enough to dump him. They can all get fucked, but I'm feeling miserable, used and desperate. I wonder how I've become this person and I don't know what to do.

We've slipped into this habit of calling in work time only and never at weekends. He comes over to see me when she thinks he's on a boy's night and only stays over when she thinks he's away with work, which has been twice.

I've turned into a person I don't want to be, to a woman that steals men, but I don't know how to stop it. I love him, and I love the sex and he makes me feel like the love of his life when we are together.

Everyone is getting sick of talking about it as well, so really, I'm alone with my pain.

But today is Friday and Juan is coming over this evening, so I have hope tonight is the night he tells me he's left her. And because it's Friday, it means work will be easier and Willy will be leaving around 3pm, leaving the rest of us to talk shit and do nothing at all.

It's also springtime in London. Everyone is smiling and being a lot nicer, so I am holding onto these thoughts when I'm feeling dark and depressed.

'So, what's everyone's plans this weekend?' I ask the team 5 seconds after Willy has left for the weekend. This starts a conversation between the 3 of us and takes us to 5 O'clock.

'I'm having a quiet one,' says Jonny.

'I'm not so busy also,' says Aggie.

'Jeez, I'm surprised at both of you, especially you Jonny, I thought you'd be shagging some beauty?' I tease, but instead of laughing and agreeing with me, Jonny seems annoyed at my accusation.

'Bree, I don't do that every weekend, hey,' Aggie and I are not convinced. Jonny isn't impressed and goes back to pretending to work.

'So Aggie, how's your love life,' implying I know something, which I don't. She shares nothing.

'Ya, things are gut. I like this one,' says Aggie, and I'm surprised. I was not expecting this.

We all knew she'd met someone at my party, and we knew she was Israeli, but she'd shared little else. I wanted more information.

'So, Smokey is a lesbian then?' I ask because I'm curious.

'Everyone is gay, Bree, don't you know,' and she winks at me, and I blush. I look away as I suddenly feel slightly uncomfortable and I don't understand why. Maybe because the porn I love to watch always involves lesbians, but that doesn't make me one, right?

'Speak for yourself, china, I much prefer pussy to cock,' pipes up Jonny.

And just like that, we are walking out of the door, wishing each other a fabulous weekend, all trying very hard not to say the dreaded M-word by saying see you on Monday.

I rush home, only stopping once at the offie to pick up a 4 pack of lager and a bottle of my favourite wine Chardonnay, ready for my night at home with Juan. I predict we'll pop to the pub for dinner, but not before we shag. It's been two weeks since we've spent a whole night together, and he's promised me 100 orgasms. I intend to make him keep his word.

And then I see the text that had been sent only 20 minutes before.

'Sorry B, something's come up. I'll call later and explain. Jx'

And just like that, everything is ruined, and I burst into tears.

But once the tears dry, and this takes a good 30 minutes of feeling sorry for myself, the rage comes flooding back in. Just a few weeks ago, I was getting over this piece of shit, yet here I am again back to the beginning of when he dumped me, and I feel wretched and determined this is the last time I will allow him to do this. And yet I know this not to be true, and I will welcome him back to my bed if he asks.

It's Friday night. I'm home alone as Jess is out for the night. I have a bottle of white wine and a few joints left in my tin which to me spells a good night in if I wasn't feeling so down. I contemplate walking to Blockbusters and hiring Friend's Season One again but can't be bothered to show my puffy face in public.

So I sit, and stew on what Juan could be doing that caused him to cancel. And as I get drunker, I get angrier, and as I get angrier, I get braver. I decide to call him, completely against the rules in case he's with her, but right now I don't care. I need answers and I want them tonight.

I ring. He doesn't answer.

I ring again, no answer.

I ring again, and this time he does.

'What the fuck Bree' he whispers through gritted teeth. I've got to him, and I'm happy.

'Baby,' I slur. 'I just needed to hear your voice. I need you tonight' in my head, I sound sexy, but realistically I sound needy, whiney and drunk.

'Look, I can't talk, ok, and Bree, you know the rules. Don't call again. I'll call you,' and he hangs up.

Motherfuckingbullshitcuntingbastard.

But I leave it because he sounded angry and over me, and I'm not ready to be dumped again.

At some stage, I stagger upstairs to bed but not before crying my eyes out and ruining Jess's night with my constant texts.

She must have come home at some stage because when I wake the next day, to cringe factor and a thumping headache, I see the note she left for me on the kitchen bench.

'Babe, don't stress, he's a first-class wanker, and you need to dump him. Love Jess xxx.'

26

It's Wednesday, and it's 9am, and I'm sitting at home about to snort my 5th line of coke today. I've been on a bender since Sunday, and I haven't been to work all week. Willy isn't happy, but he showed some sympathy when I told him. He'd rather I stay at home to process what has happened rather than sit at my desk crying like a blubbering baby all day and distracting the team.

'I'll tell Jodie you have your monthlies,' said Willy as a way of explaining my breakdown.

'No Willy, just tell her the truth,' I cry between sobs. He hung up quite quickly after that, so who knows what he's told Jodie.

My idea of processing is snorting coke, drinking Jack Daniels, smoking 20 cigarettes a day as well as weed and listening to the saddest songs I can find. You see, I don't care about myself right now and wish I was anywhere but here in London. The Greek Islands would be nice, fuck even a trip to Amsterdam would be good. I decide that is where I'm going next weekend even though I have no money due to all the coke, spliff and booze I've bought, but first, I must process this shit.

So, what is my shit? Well, it's Juan, of course. It started Friday night with the text he sent saying he couldn't make our planned night. To say I was disappointed was an understatement, but I got through the night with a lot of wine and spliff, and I waited all the next day for his call to explain why. It didn't come.

Jess and I had spent the day cleaning the house, listening to music and just being with each other, something we'd missed over the last few weeks due to parties, Juan, and other distractions, but I was on edge and I didn't leave my phone the whole day.

'Babe, he's with Bitchface, you can't wait for him. Let's go out somewhere tonight?' but I wasn't in the mood and against my better judgement, wanted to sit at home with my mobile waiting, hoping he'd call to say he was coming over.

But Jess kept insisting that I go out, and eventually we agreed on the Stag just around the corner on Acton Lane. The place was busy as there had been football on and the mood was jolly and uplifting and, for a while, I forgot that I was waiting for Juan to call me.

Around 10pm, I'd had enough. I wanted to go home and smoke a spliff and go to sleep, but Jess had met a group of people off to the Captain Cook's and told me to text when I got home and that she might be back by the morning. She winked a hopeful wink and I assumed she had her eye on one of the guys she'd met.

I'd walked home as fast as I could as I didn't want to be walking past the Swan pub at closing time and I was just desperate to get to bed as I was emotionally exhausted. As I walked around the corner and onto Antrobus Road, I could see a figure of someone outside my house. My stomach did a flip when he stepped into the lamplight and I could see it was Juan. A massive smile spread across my face and my tiredness/grumpiness disappeared instantly, I almost ran into his arms.

He embraced me in the way only he can do and kissed me so deep and passionately we almost had sex there and then in the garden, against my front door. We did not talk; we just made our way upstairs and made love. And I really mean this. I don't normally make love, but I did that night. It was slow, intense with amazing eye contact and deep, passionate, kissing. Normally we fuck hard and fast like animals, but this night was so different.

When we had finished, we lay in each other's arms until we fell asleep. Believe me, it was straight out of a Mills and Boons book! It was magical and I didn't want it to end.

When we woke the next morning early, the mood was different. As I turned over to snuggle into him, he moved away quickly and used the toilet as an excuse. I was still in the love bubble from the night before, so I didn't take it personally and proceeded to roll a joint ready for his return.

'I don't have time for that babe, I've got to go,' said Juan as he walked back into my room and saw me smoking in bed.

'Surely you have time for a puff, babe,' I said in my sexiest voice, but he was having none of it and started to get dressed.

'Hey, what happened Friday? Boy's night?' I teased.

'No, Charlene wanted to go out and I couldn't get out of it.' The reference to Bitchface stabbed me in the heart, and he must have seen my face.

'Look Bree, things are complicated right now; we've had to set a date for the wedding as her parents need to plan their flights and other stuff.'

He said it so casually and so unexpectedly that it took a few seconds to register what I'd just heard him say.

'What did you just say?' I stammered when the news eventually registered in my brain.

'What did you just say?' I repeated when I didn't get an answer.

'Don't start yeah, I've enough on my plate without you getting all emotional and shitty. You knew this was going to happen. It's just been brought forward by a few months, that's all.'

He barely got the last sentence out before I jumped up out of bed and punched him in the face, screaming like the maddest woman on the planet.

'GET OUT OF MY FUCKING HOUSE, YOU CUNT' I screamed and then spat on him, slapped him and punched him.

Juan was white with fear and hatred, and at one stage, he slapped me back, but not hard enough to stop me from raining punches into him and pulling his hair.

Jess had run into the room by this stage and was dragging me away, and this gave Juan a chance to escape my total meltdown. He offered to call me later when I'd 'calmed down', but I was never going to calm down ever, and as he left the room, I vomited all over my bed.

So, this is my poor little me story, and it's been three sleeps since it happened and no, I haven't heard from him. The rage and sadness have come over me like a heavy blanket, and I can't shake it. I'm on self-destruct. I was just getting over him when he came back into my life and I'm back to square one, but this time it feels so much more painful.

This week isn't about getting over him. This week is about hurting myself because I feel worthless and embarrassed. I can tell Jess is concerned because she's been home every night this week, which is not like her. She's also concerned that the new flatmate isn't going to want to live with a crying, psycho bitch.

'I'll be fine,' I lie that evening when Jess asks if I need to check myself into a clinic of some sort.

'Listen Bree, I really feel you need to get out of London for a while. Can you not ask your mum and dad for the money? We could pop over to Greece for a week.'

Jess had been throwing suggestions out there for a few days, and she was right. I did need to get away.

'I'm sure Acton will manage without you for a week Bree, I'd bring you to Berlin if I could, but now isn't the right time,' Jodie said when she'd called to give me her pep talk about how all men were bastards and I was better off without him.

So, I'd plucked up the courage to call Mother and she was so lovely and understanding when I cried for over an hour. Even Father had got on the phone to tell me to 'keep my chin up', and he rarely said that kind of cliched stuff.

'Look darling, find somewhere relatively cheap, and we'll pay, call it an early birthday present,' she had said, even though my birthday was months away.

'Thanks, mum, leave it with me. I'll get back to you with a destination,' and for the first time in a week, I felt something that wasn't misery.

27

He didn't remember how it started, but he knows he's enjoying himself far more than he'd like to admit.

They had started kissing in the taxi, and before he knew what was happening, he was in The Man's apartment and they were ripping each other's clothes off.

And just like that, he was standing naked in front of The Man, who had a massive hard-on, so he starts to slowly massage it as he kisses him deeply, pushing him up against the wall of the hallway.

He could feel the pleasure racing through his own body as the strokes of his hand start to speed up, and he can feel The Man's pleasure rising up through his cock and out onto his hand. They are breathing quickly from the excitement of it all, and instead of going flaccid, The Man's cock remains hard.

The Man laughs at the shock on his face and starts to return the favour, but with his mouth. And he thinks this is the best blowjob he's ever had and never wants it to end, but it does, and way too quickly for his liking.

The rest of the night surprises him beyond his wildest dreams, and before the sun comes up, they've had sex several times with no end in sight. This has been the best sex he's ever had in all his life, and it is with The Man.

Before leaving to go home a few hours later, he tells The Man he wants it again.

'I know you do, and you will,' says The Man and he leaves with a smile on his face.

28

'We're going to Kefalonia,' I tell Jess on the phone.

'Where?' she says, confused.

'Kefalonia, Greece. If we can fly out this Sunday, I can get us a week for £200 each.' Ever since Mother had offered to pay, I had been scouting the TNT and local newspapers for a good deal. I'd come across one right here in Chiswick with Tapestry Holidays.

The lady who took my call had explained that if we could leave on the 10am Sunday flight out of Gatwick, she'd sell us a room at one of their hotels in Lassi, Kefalonia. It is the best deal I can find. Mother has already agreed to pay them directly.

'Ok, do it, book it, and I'll pay your mum back in cash.'

So the deal is done and we are set to leave this Sunday, which couldn't come quick enough.

I have been stumbling through the week and the team has been very supportive of me, but I am still an emotional wreck however, but have made a point not to talk about it, mainly because I know everyone is sick of it, me included.

'You are lucky,' says Aggie.

'Come back happy, my sunshine,' says Jonny.

'Come back and never mention that name again?' says Willy.

And I agree to come back my fabulous, post-Juan self, and I promise to send a postcard, which I know I won't.

We leave tomorrow for our flight to Kefalonia and Sam, our new flatmate, is gutted he'll be left alone for a week.

'I really wanted to party with you both, but I suppose it will have to wait until you return,' he says sadly.

'You don't have to wait a week, darling, let's party tonight,' I say, hopeful, but Jess looks unsure and reminds us we have a 2.5-hour flight tomorrow, but when the hell has that ever stopped us.

'Shall I call Pablo?' I whisper to Sam, who had already been introduced to him in the week when he needed weed.

Sam nods discreetly, and I go upstairs to make the call.

He answers first ring, 'How can I help you today, gorgeous' I love the fact my dealer has my number saved in his phone.

'Um, the usual, one white t-shirt and maybe a few paracetamols,' I don't need to say more. He promises to come over within the hour.

Pablo never disappoints, and I mean never. He comes within the hour, sits in our lounge and has a beer, before moving off to service his other clients. He's expecting a busy night with the warmer weather upon us.

We drop a pill each, snort a line or two and end up having an amazing house party, just the 3 of us. We really get to know Sam as we talk a million miles an hour as we come up from the E's.

Sam is gay, 23 and originally from York. He has wanted to move to London since leaving school, but only found the opportunity recently. He works in a men's retail shop in Hammersmith, but his dream is to be Cabin Crew for Virgin. He also wants to be a Chef (he's confused) and because of the latter has offered to cook for us every night. We are thrilled we've finally found a great flatmate.

We dance, we sing, and we don't sleep, and before we know it, the taxi arrives to take us to Gatwick.

'Fuck,' I mumble as I stumble around, trying to pack in the 5 minutes I have before the taxi will leave without me.

We ride to Gatwick, coming down from the pills and quite sleepy, but we are excited to be on our way to finally get some decent sun and get away from London for the next few days.

By the time we get on the flight, we both fall asleep before the plane has taken off and don't wake up until we've landed in Kefalonia and everyone is vacating the aeroplane.

We are the last to leave the plane, and as we descend the steps onto the tarmac, we are hit with the smell of pine, jasmine and the summer heat of Greece, and it feels so good to be abroad.

While on the coach, on our way to the hotel, the Rep is giving us a mini tour of the island and points out landmarks, beaches, and pubs he recommends. After an hour and 3 stops, we finally get to our hotel, which looks modern and clean and just what we need.

Before we leave the coach and check-in, he is reminding us of the 'welcome meeting' we are all expected to attend this evening in the lobby of the hotel. Our plan today is to hit the beach, start getting our very white bodies brown and to get shit faced drunk in a local taverna. We have no intention of being at the welcome meeting but assure him we will be as we rush off to get our holiday started.

When we finally get to our room, we are not disappointed. As we open the balcony door, we are greeted with the most amazing view of azure blue waters and parts of Lassi town.

We crack open the bottle of Jack Daniels purchased in Duty-Free and sit on the balcony and take it all in. After several cigarettes and 4 large bourbons, we get into our bikinis and head off to the local beach, found right out the front of our hotel.

We spend a few hours getting brown/reddish before heading back to the room to shower and get ready for the evening. What actually happens is we finish off the bottle of bourbon and because we are still so fucked from our last night in London, we pass out early! Tomorrow we will party hard like we know we can.

29

We are currently lying on Myrtos Beach on the island of
Kefalonia and life could not be better. Well, it could be, Juan
could have left Charlene and be lying next to me now, but apart
from that, life is good.

We've been on Kefalonia now for 3 days, and I have to say, it's
one of the most beautiful places on earth. I haven't been many
places, but this Island is as beautiful as Australia.

Stunning white beaches, crystal clear blue waters and the locals
are hot, and I mean hot. The second night we ended up in a little
place called The Draught Bar in Lassi and the place rocked with
the Holiday Reps that work here. They are mad party animals, so
much fun and they all seem to be from either Manchester or
Scotland.

There are no drugs on the island, and that suits us well. The
comedown from Saturday knocked us bandy and it took a big
sleep to get over that. I ended up shagging someone from
Manchester and Jess shagged a Geordie, both Reps, and we ended
up back at their place, which they shared, a 2-bedroomed villa

next to the beach. At least they had separate rooms. We had both snuck out together in the early hours of the morning and drove our moped back to our hotel, giggling at the night we had just had and both agreeing that the sex had been awesome. We also agreed that we didn't want to see them again and they probably had no intention of shagging us again either. There are way too many options to choose from for all of us.

'Do you fancy driving over to Melissani Lake tomorrow' inquires Jess.

'Yeah, if I'm not too hungover,' I agree. So that's our plan for tomorrow and I can't wait. I wish I were a Holiday Rep now and think I might apply for a job for next season. They have the best time in the best places. Who wouldn't want to be one!

After a morning of sunbathing we go back to our room, have an afternoon siesta and get ready for another big night on the town.

We decide we are going to try the town of Argostoli as there are several restaurants and bars surrounding the main square. We choose a quiet and small Italian just tucked in one of the corners of the square and order two pizzas and a carafe of wine.

'That place looks good over there. I've been watching it fill up,' says Jess, who has just finished her food and wine and looking to get moving.

'Let's try it out,' and off we head to a lively pub called Rumours with a DJ and a dance floor. What more can two girls need.

And then I spot him sitting outside, smoking a cigarette and chatting quietly with a friend. He is sitting at one of the tables found outside of the bar and he looks at me as I walk by. He's moody looking (like most Greek men), has piercing brown eyes (again, a very Greek man trait) and the whitest of teeth. We both smile as I walk past and I know his eyes are following me to see where I sit.

Jess has missed the whole interaction as I grab her arm and steer her to a table not too far behind him. She looks at me quizzically, and I indicate with my eyes Moody Man and she understands.

We wait for the waiter to come and take our order and all the time, my eyes are boring into Moody Man's head, and just as I thought he would, he changes position to sit on the other side of the square table so that he has a sideways view of me.

I laugh, he laughs, and I know this is the man I'm going to sleep with tonight.

He eventually finds an excuse to come over to our table and we start talking. He owns a small bar in Lassi and I'm invited to join him for a drink later, once I'd finished hanging out in Argostoli. He indicates that Jess is more than welcome to join us. Moody Man buys us a round of drinks before leaving, which is very impressive and reiterates he'd like to see me in his bar later.

Now how can a girl refuse that? And I owe him one for the drinks.

We have a dance inside the pub, but Jess can tell I'm itching to get to Moody Man's bar, so we dance until the end of the song, Torn by Natalia Imbruglia, down our drinks, jump on the moped and head to Lassi.

The night is warm and the drive through the town, over the hill and into Lassi is a pleasure. We laugh at the number of mozzies and bugs that hit our faces as we speed along the busy roads. Everyone is out at this time of night. Greece does not sleep unless it's siesta time.

The bar is small and crowded and the music is chilled and mellow. The Doors are currently playing. I instantly like the vibe and Jess agrees it's chilled and the perfect place to end our night.

Moody Man is sitting at a large table at the back, to the left of the bar and he is surrounded by a small group of friends. His eyes light up when he sees us and indicates for me to come and sit next to him. He whispers something to the man sitting next to him, who looks over and smiles. Hopefully, he's just told his mate he's going to fuck me good tonight, but I'm unsure and feel slightly self-conscious.

'Hey, Bree, come sit here,' he pats the seat next to him and Jess and I squeeze ourselves onto the bench seat. He shouts something in Greek to the barman and turns back to me. He has an intense stare and a beautiful mouth. I want to kiss it now but know the night is too young.

The drinks arrive, cocktails, and the second part of our night begins. We are making small talk and Jess is being chatted up by one of Moody Man's friends who is sitting opposite her. I can tell by her hair flicking and giggling that she's interested, which is good because I want to get out of here soon and get laid.

After a few drinks and lots of conversation, he leans in to kiss me. It's slow and his large tongue pushes into my mouth deeply. I take this as a good sign that he'll be using it on me later.

By the time he suggests going back to his place, I'm quite drunk and stagger against the table. Whatever was in those drinks was strong, but I'm happy.

'Are you OK, Bree?' Jess asks, concerned, but she knows I can look after myself, and she is just checking in.

'I'll take good care of her, please don't worry, and I'll get her home in one piece,' says Moody Man as reassurance.

He guides me through the bar and out onto the road and into his car that is conveniently parked outside. It's a Mercedes and I know this man has money. I'm not interested in that; I'm interested in his tongue.

We drive for a short distance along the main road and turn left and make the ascent up the hill. The road is winding towards the top, and I'm hoping we will arrive at his place soon. It's a beautiful, sprawling villa at the top of the hill with panoramic views across the Mediterranean Sea. It's breath-taking, and I briefly wonder how many other tourists have been lucky enough to look at this view from his house.

We move into his lounge and he starts to kiss me again, deeply, but with a sense of urgency, I hadn't felt at the bar. I push him away and tell him I want a drink.

He pours us both a whiskey and leads me outside to the veranda, and we lie on the two sun loungers that are placed next to the pool. He isn't interested in talking and comes and sits next to me and pushes me back against the lounger to kiss me more. He finds my breast under my crop top and starts stroking my nipple until it hardens. I moan slightly as the pleasure courses through my body.

Whilst still kissing me, he starts to stroke my bare leg, first the outside and then he starts on my inner thigh. He is slow and gentle and he certainly knows what he is doing. By the time his hand finds my knickers, I am soaking wet and ready to be touched.

Disappointingly he stops, and I open my eyes and plead with him to keep going, but he has something else on his mind. He pulls my knickers down and takes them off, pushes the sun lounger all the way down, so I am lying on my back. He opens my legs wide and puts his mouth directly over my pussy. He does this all so quickly; I'm caught off guard and the feeling of intense pleasure hits me like a brick to the face and I groan loudly. His tongue goes deep inside me before finding my clit. He flicks it gently for a few seconds before I climax, my hands deep in his hair, pushing his face deep into me. The orgasm keeps going and I keep him there for a few seconds afterwards.

He comes up for breath, as do I, and he is smiling with his wet chin on display. I kiss him passionately, licking my juices off his face and loving the taste of me. He picks me up and takes me inside, completely knickerless and places on the sofa. He stands in front of me, and I can see his bulging cock against his trousers. I beg him to give it to me, so he starts to undo them and release it to me.

His house is in darkness, so at first, I don't quite understand what is happening, but as he pushes my face to take his cock in my mouth, it just doesn't feel right. I start to slide my mouth down the shaft of his cock and it is then I realise it is bent. Not bent like a banana like some cocks, but completely bent in the middle, as if he'd slammed it in the door and I don't know what to do.

I try my best to give his bent knob a blowjob, but after a few strokes, I start to get neck pain. He must have realised and pulls me up and bends me over and takes me from behind. But this is worse. It keeps slipping out, and it starts to feel awkward. I try to enjoy the sex, but I feel extremely uncomfortable with the constant tutting from him when it pops out. I am so glad when it's over and suggest he takes me home.

We don't say a word on the drive home, and I wonder again tonight, how many other tourists have been disappointed after a session with bent knob Moody Man.

When I get back to the room, I am so relieved to see Jess is home, awake and on her own. I couldn't wait to tell her. And we spend the next hour laughing at my bad experience.

'He could have fucked me round a corner' is our favourite saying. I did feel a bit bad taking the piss out of someone who was quite clearly deformed.

I don't see Moody Man for the rest of our trip and we avoid his bar for the rest of the week, which is easy as there are so many other places to go.

Our trip to the Lake is spectacular, and we also visit Fiscardo. Each night we eat and drink somewhere different and we end up not shagging anyone else for the rest of the holiday, which is surprising really as we are both slutty horn bags.

Overall, apart from Bent Knob, the week has been fabulous. I can highly recommend Kefalonia as one of the best places on earth and one I intend to visit again.

And I haven't talked about Juan once.

30

Sam's life had been a mess for quite a few years and he needed to get out of York as soon as possible. He really did feel like the only gay in the village, and he'd had enough of keeping his sexuality a secret. His parents had uneasily accepted it, but York itself hadn't, though it has been getting better for the gays now that it is the 90's. His love life had been very hit and miss and he believed moving to the bright lights of London would be what he needed.

He had arrived in London in the mid-'90s and had a wild time; in fact, his time in London had been too wild, and he feared for his health. Too many drugs and a lot of sex. Going to the gay clubs and bars had been a breath of fresh air for Sam and being openly gay had been liberating. By the time 1999 had come along, he was desperate to get out of his flat share in Central London with 2 other men and get to the suburbs where it might not be quite as wild.

When he'd seen the advert in the TNT for a room to rent in Chiswick with 2 females, he had called the number and clicked instantly with Jess. When he had met Bree, it felt like he was home.

It took a while to get used to the quiet life in the burbs, especially when the girls ran off to Greece without him, but he starts to enjoy his own company and finds that he can still party hard as Bree and Jess made sure of that, but he did it safely and not as crazily as he did when he lived in the city.

He makes his room comfortable and welcoming and enjoys Chiswick and West London as much as he can, occasionally going into the city and the many gay pubs when he's had enough of being surrounded by breeders, but most of his days and weekends are spent hanging out with the girls and partying quietly at home with them.

He is starting to feel happy with where he is living and the job he is in, now he just needs to find a man.

Sam is superstitious and doesn't believe someone can get this lucky and stay this lucky for long, so he decides he is going to enjoy every moment of every day until it all goes tits up and he's back to square one.

31

I've been back from Kefalonia for just over a week, Juan has not called me and it's exactly what I like. Well, sort of. I had checked my phone the minute we had landed at Gatwick, expecting to see all his texts come in, but he hadn't sent one. But as the team at Man Source have pointed out, it is the only way I'm going to get on with it.

Willy is happy I'm back and emotionally stable. Jodie is happy I'm back and recruiting staff. Jonny is happy I'm back because he now has someone to talk to, and Aggie doesn't seem to care that I'm back. I don't think she even noticed I had gone.

'Ya, I noticed, coz I had to answer more calls' was the only affectionate thing she said to me when I returned.

I bore the team with my stories of Kefalonia, but they all laugh at Bent Knob.

'Uck man, you have the worst luck,' says Jonny.

'Yuck,' says Aggie.

'I'd have found a way,' says Willy.

'Hey, do you want to go to a party on Saturday night,' says Jess while we are sitting in the garden smoking spliffs.

It is a balmy June evening in London and the weather is fabulous. We still have nice deep tans from our week in Kefalonia and we are admiring our long brown legs as we talk.

'Who's and where?' I ask.

'Pablo said that Acacia Road is having one of their parties and we should go.'

Acacia Road parties are infamous and Jess and I had been trying to get an invite to one of them for a while. Of course Pablo services them and when we'd found that out recently, we'd told him to let us know when they were having another one.

He'd texted Jess to tell her Saturday was the night and as we'd been keen to attend one, we decided that Saturday it would be.

We order our drugs, 4 pills and a gram of coke and look forward to it with only three nights to wait.

'What are you going to wear,' I ask Jess as we start to get ready for the Acacia Road party.

'I'm thinking crop top and skirt' and I decide to wear the same. London is too hot right now to be in jeans which is my favourite piece of clothing.

Pablo pops around and drops off his goods and he let us know, as he always does, that these are the best pills on the market right now. He is usually spot on with his recommendation and we are excited to drop them. I don't want to take them before getting there as I want to check out the crowd first.

We stop at The Stag on the way up Acton Lane and have a couple of pints of cider and then carry on walking up to Acton High Street. We turn right onto the High Street and then a left onto Grove, then a right onto Churchfield and a final left onto Myrtle, which will eventually take us to Acacia. It's quite a long walk, but with a few drinks inside us, we enjoy the trip.

We can hear the music before turning onto Acacia and it is obvious which house it is. The amount of people spilling out onto the pavement and road gives it away. At least fifty men and woman, in all states, were laughing, dancing and singing, and it isn't even 7pm. I'd hate to be one of their neighbours.

I don't recognise anyone and I'm not sure this is going to be my thing. We make our way past everyone, saying hi to those who look interested and into the house, which is heaving. I'm shocked at the number of people who are in the house and I'm also shocked at how many mattresses are piled up behind the sofa, indicating how many people actually live here. There are people everywhere. We snake our way through to the back garden and the party is really in full swing.

I open a can of cider I've been carrying and stand in a spot that is free and start to talk to Jess. 'Shall we stay?' I ask. Hoping she'll say no, let's go home, but she's happy to be there. More so than me.

'Give it time, Bree, I'm sure we'll see someone we know,' and we do. Pablo. But he's busy doing the rounds and selling his gear to even notice us.

'Let's drop a pill and see where this takes us,' says Jess, but I'm nervous about taking class A's with people I don't know. I'm not sure why I've started to feel uneasy in crowds of strangers, but just lately it bothers me.

'Hi, who are you,' says a spaced out Kiwi guy. He is nice, but he can barely string a sentence together, so I don't try to explain who we are. He eventually moves on when he realises we are not engaging.

We wait for the pills to kick in, just milling around and trying to decide if we are enjoying ourselves when eventually they do, and they don't disappoint. I'd been nervous and shy when I had first walked in, but now I'm talking to everyone and dancing my tits off on the makeshift dance floor that was once the lounge.

I meet some interesting people tonight and I even have a good conversation with Kiwi guy. Still, I am not interested in anything other than having a good laugh, some dancing and drinking and meeting new people. I politely decline a couple of kisses that come my way and I go home with Jess, manless.

We walk back to our house in Chiswick, purely because we are still high as kites and have the energy of marathon runners. By the time we get back to Antrobus Road, we are exhausted and ready to smoke a spliff and come down, not surrounded by strangers with Friends on loop. Sam is out, so we have the house to ourselves, like old times. The perfect way to end the night.

32

Today is the 29th of June 1999, exactly 5 days until Juan says, 'I do', and I feel my chances of stopping the wedding are zero. Juan had texted me a couple of weeks ago, to give me a 'heads up' about the wedding as he didn't want me hearing it from someone else, dick.

I have texted and called him several times over the last couple of weeks, not proud of myself, but I wanted to hear from him, for him to say it had been cancelled and he was coming back.

He took one of my calls and was cold and angry with me.

'Look, Bree, just stop with the fucking calls. Yeah, if she finds out, she'll fucking kill me.'

'I just want you to tell me you are getting married, and we are over, ok' I had pleaded. I sounded pathetic.

'What the fuck do I have to do to convince you, Bree,' he explodes. 'I'm getting married, just leave me alone, ok? I can't deal with you right now,' and he hung up.

I have cried an ocean of misery and I don't know how I'm going to get through this week. I can't believe I still have a job either. I've called in sick several times and I'm still on self-destruct. I've lost a stone (yay), spent all my money on coke (boo), and everyone I know has lost complete patience with me. They've had enough but don't understand the pain I'm in.

Going to Kefalonia helped, but the grief came back tenfold when I realised that the 3rd of July at Ealing Registry Office was going to go through. Unless a meteorite hits at that exact time, nothing was going to stop the wedding.

I have been having thoughts and dreams of stopping the wedding. Just as the registrar asks, 'Is there anyone here who believes this wedding should not go through' I storm through the doors shouting, 'Yes, stop, he loves me, not her.' But I'm not sure if this is even asked at a civil ceremony or whether it just happens at a church wedding. It does not stop me from dreaming of doing it though.

When I share my idea with the team, they are all horrified. Jess was mortified for me and begged me not to do anything stupid.

'Let's make a plan to stay busy this Saturday Bree, let's go into the city and shop,' she had suggested.

Nope, I intend to be in Ealing that day. I need to see it for my own eyes. It's not over till it's over. And I also want to feel more misery.

'So, team, I have some news from Jodie,' Willy says at our team meeting. I'm not paying much attention, I'm hungover again, and I'm thinking three more sleeps, three more sleeps.

'Berlin is ramping up for the summer period and they've had an influx of English speakers into the area. Jodie needs help processing from her end. She wants one of you there next week for a 2-week secondment and I'm thinking you might need this trip, Bree.'

I hear my name, but I've missed the beginning of the conversation, and I look at Willy with a blank expression.

'Lucky bitch,' mumbles Aggie.

'That will be good for you, bru,' says Jonny.

'What?' I say blankly.

'You are leaving for Berlin this weekend, Bree. Jodie needs you over there for two weeks.'

'Um no, I can't leave this weekend, Willy, I'm um busy,' I lie.

'Why, what are you doing?' asks Willy, but he knows what I want to do because I'd already told him.

I don't answer, so he carries on.

'It's not a request, babe, it's an order, but if you can't fly out Saturday, I'll book your flight for Sunday,' his eyes implore. He doesn't want to risk making me cry or having a meltdown and I know he's been talking to Jodie, and they believe getting me out of London will help me get over it all.

'Can I think about it?'

'No,' says Willy in such a way I know the conversation is over.

'Can I go outside and die' I mouth, and he nods me towards the courtyard.

'Look Bree, Jodie and I agree it would be best if you get out of town for a while. You are literally falling apart in front of me and I'm worried for you, darl.'

I cry at his kindness and he even gives me a hug. I'm surprised. Willian doesn't do affection or touching of any kind that isn't sex. It makes me cry more and I feel his sympathy.

191

'You are skin and bone, Bree, you need to fix yourself' I'm happy that he thinks I'm skin and bone and feel a flash of joy at the compliment.

'Thanks Willy.'

'It wasn't a compliment,' says William worriedly.

We finish dying and move back into the office, where Willy proceeds to book my flight to Berlin and call Jodie to let her know what time I'm arriving.

'She gets into Tegal at 6.30pm, darl. Be sure to meet her,' he instructs Jodie.

And with that, I have a flight booked to Berlin, 24 hours after Juan's wedding.

I'm sitting on the couch with Jess later that night, smoking a spliff and feeling a bit more mellow and we've been talking about my trip to Berlin.

'I think it's a good thing Bree and Berlin rocks.'

Jess has been to Berlin twice and loves the place. She's written down a list of places I need to visit.

'Yeah, I suppose so, though I don't feel ready to mingle and socialise.' My idea of socialising right now has been to snort coke on my own in my room. Not the best thing for me, but I've enjoyed wallowing in misery whilst high.

'I'm just going there to help process the workers, I'm not going out. I'm just going to sit in my hotel and sleep and heal myself,' I say to Jess. We both start laughing at how ridiculous I sound, and we both know that is never going to happen.

'Mate, that city *never* sleeps, you'll be out every night, and you never know, you might meet Heir Flick while you're there.' We laugh our stoned laugh because we both know I want to meet a German so I can tick that country off my list.

33

So, the day has finally come for Juan and Charlene's wedding.
The day I have been working so hard to stop since I arrived back
from Australia all those months ago. When the weather was
crappy and cold, the nights were dark and long and when I had
hope that this day would never come.

I don't know how I'm feeling. Numb. Sad. Still slightly hopeful.
Jess has gone into the city as planned and I'm sitting here with
Sam, smoking a spliff and contemplating my day.

'Well, I think you should go and stand outside the registry office
and wait,' says Sam. I like Sam. He has been the only one out of
my circle of friends who isn't sick of me talking about it and who
has encouraged me to do everything I can to stop the wedding.

Jess says the only reason he isn't sick of hearing about Juan is
because he's only been hearing about him for a few weeks,
whereas everyone else has had to listen to me go on and on for
months.

'Get yourself dressed up looking hot and sexy, grab a coffee and
20 fags and go sit your arse outside for as long as you need, babe.

I'm happy to come with you. I've no plans,' says Sam as an afterthought.

'Would you?' I ask, hopefully.

'Of course, gorgeous, you can't do this shit on your own.'

And with that I have a partner in crime to come and sit with me, in the beautiful July sun, to stop Juan's wedding.

I'm excited because I've been scared to do this on my own and now, I have Sam and I'm feeling a lot more confident.

I rush to get ready as I don't know the time of the wedding and plan to do exactly what Sam has suggested; find a bench to sit on, close enough to the registry office so I can see who comes and goes and watch and wait. Drinking wine, not coffee, smoking spliff and ciggies. The perfect way to spend a Saturday.

I put on my shortest skirt (Juan loved me in short skirts, it gave him quick access), the tightest top to show off my tits (Juan loved my tits), flip flops on the feet and a bit of lippy and mascara, and I'm ready to roll.

Sam approves as I walk down the stairs and whistles at me as if he is a straight workman on a building site.

'I'd fuck you babe if I didn't like cock.'

'I know darling, I'd fuck you too if you didn't like cock so much.'

We head out to the station, walking to Acton Town instead of Chiswick Park and take the train to Ealing Broadway. Once we get there, we turn left out of the station and make the short walk to the registry office.

I have butterflies in my stomach. What if I've missed them (not possible, it's only 8.30am), what if he sees me (a possibility for sure) and what if he stops the wedding before it happens (slim chance).

Sam is reading my mind, I'm sure, and he holds my hand as reassurance that he's here for me. I feel blessed and lucky that this amazing human has come into my life and my heart feels a lot of love for him right now.

We stop at Café Nero, as it's a tad too early for wine, get our takeaways and find the perfect bench to make our home for the next few hours. On the other side of the road, opposite the registry office, which is a grand, beautiful building, is a row of benches. I choose the one where I have the best view of the place and park myself down.

I've rolled us 4 joints for the day and I also have half a gram of coke, already beautifully cut up and ready to be snorted from the nasal machine I have for times when I'm on the go. Today could just turn out to be a good day.

And so the wait begins. We chat, laugh and watch as groups of wedding guests start to arrive for the first service. I scan the crowd to see if I can see anyone I know, but I recognise nobody. Every time someone turns up, I start to feel sick, and by 11am and 3 groups of weddings later, there is still no sign of Juan and Charlene's party.

'I think it's time for wine,' I declare to Sam after our 3rd coffee and 2 spliffs. I also want some coke. So, I discreetly have a snort, as does Sam, and go off to the corner shop for a bottle of Chardonnay.

I rush back as I don't want to miss anything, but Sam assures me no other party has arrived. We watch as the 3rd happy couple descend the steps to a shower of confetti and lots of happy, smiling people congratulating them.

There seems to be a lull in the ceremonies, so we continue to drink wine, smoke and talk and laugh about what a great day we are having and then, as I look over to the other side of the road, I see someone who looks familiar and I stop talking and stare. Sam can feel my energy change and looks towards the couple I'm staring at.

It isn't Juan, but it's one of his friends and his girlfriend. She's dressed in a beautiful summer dress with flowers all over it and thin straps that show off her slim body. He's dressed in a tailored navy suit, with a crisp white shirt and paisley tie. They are holding hands and marching towards the registry office as if they are late.

I slump down onto the bench, ready to witness what is obviously about to happen. Not long after the first couple arrive, more start to come. Most of them young and beautiful and all in a happy joyous mood.

Within 20 minutes, there is a large crowd gathered on the steps and they are looking in the direction of Acton, waiting for the wedding car I assume.

Sam and I don't talk. I'm trying to take in all the faces, scanning the crowd for you know who. My heart is racing. I don't want to be seen, but at the same time, I cannot move from this spot.

And then the white Limousine arrives and my stomach lurches towards my mouth. It takes all my will power not to throw up as I watch an older couple get out, looking very polished and preened, ready for their daughter's wedding, because it must be her parents. Juan's aren't coming.

Out step the bridesmaids—two of them. I recognise one of them. I have seen her at the Redback on several occasions. I hold my breath and out he steps. Juan. He looks back at the car with his hand outstretched and helps pull out his bride to be, who is wearing a simple white dress, more for a cocktail night than a wedding, and she looks stunning. Her shiny black hair flows down her back and off her face and she looks happy and radiant. Exactly how a bride should look.

Charlene looks around the crowd and greets people with warm hugs and kisses whilst Juan shakes hands and pats backs, and then they start to climb the steps to the registry office so that they can say 'I do'.

I catch my breath in my throat and my knees are weak. I will him to look around and see me standing on the other side of the road. If he's seen me, he makes no indication of it and I watch them all walk into the building as I sit back down on the bench.

Sam touches my arm gently and breaks my trance. I burst into tears and sob quietly against his shoulder.

'Come, let's go home, Bree,' he says.

'No, Sam, I've come this far; I want to see them when they come out.'

He looks pained and seems to be regretting his suggestion to sit here for the day. I sniff loudly to clear my nose because I want another hit of coke. I take a hit and drink a large swig from the wine. We are about to run out and Sam suggests buying another one.

'Yes please,' I say miserably. I can't possibly run to the shop because I don't want to miss the finale.

Sam runs to the shop and makes it back in less than 5 minutes with another bottle of cold Chardonnay and I'm grateful he is here with me.

'Thank you for being with me today, Sam,' and he cuddles me hard and tight.

We sit back on the bench and wait for the final chapter of this sad, pathetic story. We've been receiving disapproving looks from some of the people who have walked past today and I really do not care.

'What shall we do tonight?' says Sam, trying to distract me.

'I've already texted Pablo to get more coke and some pills,' I say.

Sam seems happy with this plan.

Less than 40 minutes after arriving, the wedding party start to make their way onto the sweeping steps of the Ealing Registry Office, making a pathway for when the happy couple descend and just like that, they are there, at the top of the steps. A married couple looking happy and flushed and holding hands. They make their way slowly down the steps, all the while being congratulated, with confetti in their hair.

I watch, like a psycho who loves pain, as they hang around for photos and small talk before their wedding car arrives to take them to whatever reception venue they have hired. I have no idea where that is and I think my wedding watching is over.

He's done it, he said I do, and there was nothing I said or did these past few months that stopped it. My stomach lurches and I throw up on the pavement in front of our bench.

This is our sign to leave and Sam guides me towards the station to get me to the safety of home, and away from the circus we have just witnessed.

Jess is home when we walk through the door and she can see from my face that it's happened, it's all over and she hugs me while whispering that I will be ok, that she is here for me, and now I can start my life again, after putting it on hold for so long.

She is right but tonight is about getting as fucked as I can and forgetting all about it.

Pablo drops off the goodies and I pop the pill as soon as it's in my hand. He knows something is up but he doesn't ask; he's there to deliver drugs, not be a counsellor and off he goes to the next customer.

The pill works well. I'm happy, ecstatic and I dance and laugh and sing with my beautiful flatmates well into the night. We go over the day as if there is no pain involved, and this is down to the chemicals racing through me. It does the trick.

I don't know what time I go to bed, but around 2pm the next day, Jess is frantically trying to wake me.

'Bree, for fuck sake, you've got a flight to catch.'

'Fuck,' I say as I wake from my drugged state. My room is a mess, I haven't packed and I must leave for Heathrow in less than an hour.

'Fuck.'

I don't know how I do it, but I manage to get my flight just in time. Feeling like a bag of shit and wanting to vomit the whole flight over, I'm dreading meeting Jodie at the airport and wish she'd just arranged a taxi, but I think she just wants to make sure I get there.

I needn't have worried; Jodie is so hungover when I eventually get to Tegal Airport that she apologises for the state she is in and promises to take me for dinner the following evening.

I am happy with that and after our 40-minute journey, with very little being said between us, I get to my serviced apartment, dump my bags at the door and go and pass out on my big queen bed the minute my head hits the pillow.

34

I wake early on this hot summer day in Berlin, and it takes a few seconds to remember where I am. Jodie had dropped me off at my serviced apartment in a place called Alexanderplatz, somewhere in East Berlin, at around 8pm. I had dumped my suitcase at the front door and made my way to the bedroom, where I am currently in bed.

I can see out of the window and I'm looking directly at the TV tower, which looks like a massive building with an onion on top. I can hear the city coming to life and the traffic can just be heard through the double glazing.

I get out of what must be the most comfortable bed I've ever slept in and I explore the flat. Nothing exciting. Lounge, kitchen and diner and a small balcony off this. It has everything I need and I'm delighted to find coffee in the cupboard and milk in the fridge.

As I wait for the kettle to boil, I check my phone. Has Juan texted me to say he's made a mistake? No, but Jodie texted late last night to tell me to be ready for 8am and outside the front of the apartment block, where she'll pick me up.

I check the time, 6.30am, plenty of time to drink coffee, smoke and get ready. I sit on the balcony and watch as Berlin comes alive on this beautifully warm Monday. I'm high up and I don't like heights, but I can see into the distance from where I'm sitting and don't look down.

I text Jess to say I've arrived safely. I text Sam and thank him again for Saturday forgetting that I am one hour ahead of them and wonder why they don't text back immediately.

I'm feeling drained from the weekend from hell. Too many drugs, too many tears and I swear to myself that I will not shed another tear over him again. I also swear to myself that I will not mention his name again. In the words of Rachel, it is time for closure. Do I believe I'll do it? Sure. Do I believe I will never mention him again? Maybe not.

I unpack the few things I threw into my suitcase yesterday while in a hurry, have a shower, get dressed and by the time I've smoked my 8th cigarette, it is time to go out onto the street and wait for Jodie.

As I walk through the double doors of the apartment block and onto the pavement, I can see she's already waiting, and I rush over.

'Sorry, Jodie, am I late?'

'Yeah nah, all good mate, I'm always early, how ya doing?'

And I find myself crying because she sounds genuinely concerned for me and she gives me a brief hug.

'Come on girl, enough of the tears and drama, okay? You have a great opportunity to get away and reset your mind. You are one of my best Bree, and I need you focussed these next two weeks. I am being slammed with workers and need you processing, okay?'

'Yeah, sorry Jodie, it's been a hard few weeks, but I promise that is the last cry ever over him, ok, I'm yours. You tell me what you need, and I'll do it.'

This is exactly what Jodie wants to hear, and she's happy. She indicates for us to get into the car and off we drive to the office. As we move through the streets of Berlin, I'm amazed at how stunning the buildings are, I'm also surprised at how many building sites and cranes can be seen across the city.

Jodie has rented a ground floor office space on Oranienburger Str opposite a place called Tacheles. 'I'll take you there while you are here; it's a great place for a drink and a smoke,' says Jodie, and I feel excited that she likes to smoke. When Jodie comes to London, she parties hard with William but never us, the workers. Willy has implied she loves them, but I'd never heard her talk about them or do them. She obviously knew about my drug-taking, though.

The office space is bright and airy, with 4 desks facing the front area and a reception area that can seat 8 people. This is where the workers come to sign up, fill in paperwork and receive their instructions on where they are to go and who to ask for.

We are alone, and Jodie indicates which desk to sit at. I settle in and offer to make us both a coffee from the kitchen, which is just an anti-room off the main space.

We both spark up our cigarettes and chat quietly about the expectations of my visit. Jodie wants me to start entering all the names and contact numbers of the workers onto a spreadsheet. If the phone rings, I'm to answer it in English, which is a good thing as I don't speak German. If any workers come into the office, she will deal with them.

And so my first day on the job in the Berlin office goes well. I complete all that is expected of me and at 3pm, I'm told I can go home.

'I'll drop you home, and then I'll meet you at Kilkenny Irish Bar at around 7 for dinner; it is literally a 5-minute walk from your apartment. Don't panic I'll point it out as we go,' says Jodie after seeing the panic on my face at the thought of walking around Berlin alone without a word of German in my vocabulary.

We drive past a large and sprawling pub on the corner at Hackescher Markt and she is right; it is a stone's throw away from my apartment block.

'Thanks Jodie, I'll see you at 7.' I jump out of the car and head up to my apartment to sleep and chill until dinnertime.

At 6.45pm I leave my apartment and walk through the streets of Hackescher Markt. It feels good to be outside. The city is literally buzzing with people, trams, cars and bicycles. It feels like a Saturday night in London, not a Monday night! I love the vibe and I'm so glad to be here and not in London.

I'd spoken to Jess just before leaving the apartment and she was having a boring night in front of the telly. Me, I am in Berlin on my way to an Irish Pub to eat dinner and drink wine.

I find Jodie sitting in the beer garden. She is sitting with four men who have quite obviously just finished work. They wear muddy work boots and dirty clothes. I greet them shyly.

'Bree, I want you to meet some of Man Source's finest,' and she proceeds to introduce me to them.

'Guys, this is Bree from the London office; she's over here to help me out for a couple of weeks.'

I don't remember their names, but they are all Irish and friendly. I'm bought a pint of cider by one of them and they move off to another table to let us talk and eat.

I order a schnitzel and chips and Jodie orders the Irish stew. It's the best one in the city, according to Jodie.

'So, this weekend is going to be crazy; you've picked a good week to come to Berlin. Have you heard of the Love Parade?' I tell her I've heard of it but didn't know it was happening this weekend.

'Yeah, it's gonna be wild; it starts Saturday, but the city will be on it from Friday. I've a few plans, but I'll be happy to show you around and take you to a few clubs. You are gonna love it. You like pills, right?' I'm unsure what to say. This is my boss and I hesitate.

'Come on Bree, Willy tells me everything.' So, I spill my guts and tell her about all the drugs I love and how I've been on a massive bender since Fucktard set the date. Fucktard is my new name for him. I can't mention him by his real name right now.

'Look, I don't particularly like class A's,' Jodie lies, 'but if that's your thing, and it doesn't affect your work, I don't really care what you do. Hell the whole of Berlin takes drugs, I will have some coke and a few pills for Love Parade, but that's it, oh, and by the way, I'm going to be busy this week, but I'm all yours from Friday, you will be fine on your own.'

We finish our meal and have a couple more drinks but then Jodie is tired and wants to go home. 'You can stay if you want, but I'm about to hit the sack,' she says in her Australian twang.

'I'm good Jodie and need to go home too. I'll see you in the morning—no need to pick me up, I'll walk to the office,' I say bravely. I'm keen to start exploring as I'm only here for a short time and it only took 5 minutes by car to get to my apartment from the office, so a nice walk in the morning will do me good.

'Ok, if you're sure, I'll see you at 8, ok, don't be late,' and before she leaves, she hands me a small bag of weed and zig-zag rolling papers.

My night has just got better and I thank her with a kiss on the cheek and rush out of the pub and over to my apartment as quickly as I can. Later that night, I smoke some of the best skunk I've ever tried and fall into a deep, no dream sleep—something I have needed for weeks.

35

I have been in Berlin for almost a week, and I am loving this city. Every night I've been somewhere different for a drink or dinner. I've tried to fit in some sightseeing after work as I know this weekend is going to be hectic with the Love Parade and I really don't want to go back to London having not seen a thing.

It has always surprised me when I meet Australians or Kiwis who have been in London for two years and travelled nowhere. Frantically booking a Contiki Tour as they are leaving the UK, just so they can tell the folks back home they've seen Europe. I don't want to be one of those tourists. I want to see the place.

I've been to East Side Gallery at the Berlin Wall and Check Point Charlie. I'm fascinated with this city and wish I could stay longer. I've drunk cider at Oscar Wildes Irish Pub and smoked a spliff with the locals at Tacheles. I'm loving the easy-going vibe of the place and could really see myself living here.

My heart is still broken into a million pieces, but I'm not here to hook up, or shag or find love, which is a complete first for me.

I'm here to work and get my head back into a healthy place. And for now, I'm going to be a tourist in this amazing city.

I've picked up a bit of German and I think Jodie is happy with the work I've been doing. She is so busy and barely in the office. When she is, she's screaming in German at some poor Construction Manager who is running a site that she has workers on. She seems stressed most of the time and chain-smokes all day, which suits me fine because that is what I like doing too.

She mentioned a boyfriend briefly on the first night at dinner but didn't go into too much detail. He works in the industry and is separated from his wife with grown-up children. I get the impression she's not that into him, but that he'll do for now.

'Ok, so this is the plan for Saturday. I'll come to yours around 9, and we'll walk to Tacheles from where we'll make our way through to the Gate and onto Tiergarten as this is where the best floats can be seen. I'll sort out the pills and coke. Dress the part, nothing fancy as you'll be a mess by the end.'

I have 2 nights to prepare for the biggest party of the year. I decide I want to take it easy and stay at home. I'm quite bored in the apartment as all the programs on TV are in German, so I spend the nights talking to Jess and my mum. I even have an hour's conversation with William who is desperate to hear how it's all going, jealous as fuck that I'm at the Love Parade this weekend.

'Nothing to report, darl, the world is still turning while you are away Bree and Acton is still the biggest shithole in London.'

'I miss you all,' I say, feeling slightly homesick.

'I might even try and fly in Saturday morning, but I think I've left it too late,' says Willy.

'I'd love to see you here,' I say, and I mean it. William is great fun, and we could do loads of damage if he were here.

He hangs up but not before telling me to try and stay alive and safe this weekend.

I decide I'm wearing my tight, white shorts that are so short my giblets can almost be seen, but as I have lovely brown legs right now from my trip to Kef, I want to show them off. I have a baby pink plain t-shirt, see-through enough that you can just make out my nipples, my hair is pulled into a high ponytail and I have some flat, strappy sandals on my feet. Limited makeup as it's a stinking hot day and I don't want mascara running down my face, but I do put on a bit of shiny lip gloss.

I have a small girly backpack on, with a packet of 20 Marlboro Lights, 200 Deutsche Marks, a bank card, weed, zig-zag papers and a lighter inside. I'll pick up water on my way and Jodie has promised to get me the pills and coke.

I'm just finalising the look when my doorbell rings. I answer and its Jodie looking damn hot and ready to party.

'Thought I'd pop up and chop us up a line before we start the walk.'

I can hear the party out on the street already and it's only 8.45am. I start to get butterflies in my stomach as the excitement begins to build.

She chops up four massive lines of coke and we put one up each nostril. I'm so fucking excited and really impressed; my boss, who has always come across as a ball-breaking bitch, seems quite nice and misunderstood.

'Remember Bree, whatever happens this weekend, you had better be in the fucking office Monday or you're fired, yeah?' Ah, and the ball breaking bitch is back, but I can see she's pulling my leg, hopefully.

'Nah, all good, babe, the office is closed Monday, your gonna need that day to chill, believe me.'

'No wonder Willy wishes he were here,' I say.

'Willy can go fuck himself; last time he was here, I didn't see him for a week.'

And off we walk down onto the street. The place is heaving with people, all smiling and happy and dressed for a techno rave at 9am on this wonderful Saturday morning.

I wonder where Jodie's friends are, and, as if she reads my mind, she tells me we'll be catching up with them all later. So we continue to walk through Hachesche Markt and onto Oranienburger Strasse. The walk is long, but we have a few lines up our nose and enjoy the walk.

The place is rocking already. There are thousands of people walking through the streets, dancing, singing and partying as if the world is ending tomorrow.

The atmosphere is electric and the mood is friendly and loving. I suspect most of the party-goers are on E's and I'm keen to join them.

'Hey, did you get any pills for this weekend, Jodie?' I ask.

'Yeah, fucking shit loads, I'll sort you out when we find a spot to park.'

And we find an amazing spot to park, as Jodie calls it. In the beer garden out the back, around all sorts of weird things coming out of the ground, including a rocket and a bus.

'We won't be staying here all day, but it's a good place to be for now,' says Jodie as we park at a table with benches and start the party.

I get a round of drinks in and when I get back to the table, it is full of Jodie's friends. I'm relieved as I was actually thinking she didn't have any as I'd seen no evidence of them. Still, there was a pleasant selection of Irish, German, Australian and New Zealand men and woman who all know her well.

We make our acquaintances and start the small talk of where are you from, what do you do etc. They all work in the construction industry in some form or another and they all seem like massive party animals. A couple of the guys are cute, but I'm not really taking much notice; however, I'm ruling nothing out.

An ecstasy pill gets given to me, not very discreetly, by the Kiwi sitting next to me. Jodie has passed it to him from across the table to give to me. I look around to see if that is what everyone else is doing and I'm informed they've all just dropped one.

It's 11am, and my first pill is inside me. My stomach does a flip, like always, and I gag slightly as it goes down. I will it to stay there as I have been known to throw them up from time to time. Not sure why. It could be my body protesting at the poison I'm making it take.

The music is pumping and I can feel the beat throbbing through my body. I can hear the party getting into full swing out on the street and the place is crammed with people. I believe every single person in Berlin right now is on pills and the thought excites me.

After about 45 minutes, I feel the familiar rush of the E coursing through my body and up into my brain, and I'm standing up to dance at the table. A smile spreads across my face, where it will stay for the next 8 hours.

It's almost simultaneous with everyone else who is sitting with me because they all stand up, start dancing, smiling, kissing and hugging. It's called the love drug for a reason and right now, I fucking love everyone!

'How you doing, gorgeous girl,' says Jodie, whose pupils are as big as her smile.

'I'm so happy Jodie, thank you so much for getting me out of London; I needed that. I love you.'

'I love you too. Let's go to the party and watch the parade.'

She indicates for us all to leave Tacheles and make our way to the Brandenburg Gate.

The walk takes us over 2 hours because of the crowds and the distance, but we spend the time laughing and talking as we go, and her friends take me under their wing as if I've been there for years.

'You like Berlin ya,' said this beautiful German guy who'd been sitting with us at Tacheles. He'd come with his girlfriend, who is equally as beautiful.

'I think it's the best city on earth,' I gush.

'Ya, so do we,' he says.

By the time we get to the Gate and Tiergarten, there must be over 2 million people, and the music is pumping. There is dancing in the street and not one person looks unhappy.

We stay and watch the floats and the night keeps going. By now I've had 3 pills and a shitload of coke. I don't want the night to end.

We spend most of the day/night at Tiergarten and around midnight we decide to head to a club called Tresor. This club rocks. Lots of underground rooms that are dark and smoky and the music is trance. I wander around the place, getting lost on my travels but eventually find my group in the garden and join them.

We are coming down from the pills by the time the sun comes up, and no one wants to go home, so we stay in the garden, smoke weed and drink water and talk about the amazing Love Parade.

'How long are ya here for Bree,' says the cute Kiwi.

'I'm going back to London next weekend.'

'You should go to the Kit Kat before you go,' he says, laughing.

'Ya, the Kit Kat is gut Bree,' says beautiful German girl.

'Ok, I will; when?'

'I'll take you next Friday,' she says.

And just like that, I have another session booked for the following weekend.

By the time I get back to my apartment, I am exhausted. My feet hurt from the walking and dancing and my cheeks hurt from all the smiling and chewing, but I have to say it was the best weekend of my life.

36

It's been hard work at the office this week, especially after such a massive weekend. I spent all of Sunday afternoon sleeping and eventually made it out of bed and down to Oscar Wilde Pub for dinner and a couple of pints of cider. I couldn't believe that the party was still going and Berlin was still rocking over 24 hours after the Love Parade had ended. Oscar Wildes was rammed with people, and everyone was still in the best mood. Lots of people still out from the day before, and it was all looking rather messy. It was fun to watch. Most people keep going until the Monday. Not me. I spent Monday lounging on the couch, smoking weed and sleeping.

Jodie was ropey on Tuesday and didn't stay in the office for long as we had no new workers coming in to register for work. I spent most of the day on the phone to the Acton office, telling them all about my weekend. Jonny didn't believe me when I said I hadn't shagged anyone. Willy didn't sound convinced either. Aggie didn't care either way.

'I've had some of the best weekends of my life in Berlin,' says William nostalgically.

'I'm jealous as hell, bru. It's quiet without you, hey,' says Jonny.

'I miss you all and can't wait for next Monday,' I lie as I really want to stay in Berlin for a bit longer.

I've been told to wear my sexiest, most revealing outfit for tonight's visit to the Kit Kat Klub and I'm hoping it's good enough. I have my shortest skirt on that doesn't show off my fanny, a crop top that shows off my flat, brown stomach whilst also making my small tits look a decent size, sandals on my feet and a lot more make up than I put on for the Parade.

I'm meeting beautiful German couple at a wine bar in the district of Kreuzberg, which is close to the club. I'm due there at 11pm and this time I'm going alone, not with Jodie. She made some excuse earlier in the week about not being able to come but to enjoy myself. I'm quite excited as I've heard it's a great club and if it's anything like Tresor, I'll be happy.

I have a pill in my purse and some coke left over from last weekend, which I feel will be enough drugs as I have a flight back to London on Sunday morning and I don't want to miss it or be a mess for when I get home.

At 10.30pm, I jump into a taxi just outside my apartment and give the driver the name of the place and location I'm going to. My bad German couldn't have been that bad because he nods his head in understanding and drives me, hopefully, in the right direction. He is from Turkey and his German is as bad as mine. I happily sit in silence all the way. My stomach is nervous.

I don't know BGC (beautiful German couple) very well, we've only really had one night to get to know each other, but they took me under their wing at the Love Parade. Their English is near perfect (of course, they are German). They are so friendly and lovely to me that I am flattered they want to show me the best nightclub in Berlin before leaving for London.

They are sitting at a table outside the bar and wave to me as I get out. Again, the place is heaving with people and it feels like this really is the city that doesn't sleep.

'Come darling, sit next to me,' says beautiful German girl (BGG) and indicates for her partner to go and get me a drink.

'You look lovely,' I say, and she does. Thin as a rake, the blackest of hair in a pixie cut and the bluest of eyes. Red lips with barely a piece of clothing on her. She has so much flesh showing, she almost looks naked.

Beautiful German Boy (BGB) comes back with my drink and gives me a peck on the cheek.

'You look ready for Kit Kat Bree, das ist gut,' he says.

'Do you know about the club' he continues.

'No, nothing really, just been told it's the best one in Berlin, and I'm dying to dance. Are you dropping tonight?' I indicate, taking a pill, and they both laugh.

They have already dropped and are ready to go clubbing and come up, so I drop mine as I want to be on the same wavelength as they are.

'You are going to love Kit Kat,' says BGG as she links my arm in hers and walks me 200 metres to the door of Kit Kat.

The bouncer stops me with his hand and looks me up and down. I'm nervous. What if I don't look cool enough for this place, or worse still, what if he knows I've taken drugs.

BGG starts speaking in German to the bouncer and he lets me pass.

'What was all that about?' I ask.

'They want to make sure you are dressed the part,' and BGG says no more.

We walk through a dark corridor and into the club, and I'm disappointed. It's quite empty and there is no one on the dance floor.

As if reading my mind, BGB says, 'It will get busier later, I promise.'

We make our way to the bar.

I offer to buy a drink; we only want water. I lean against the bar and then I notice the bar staff. The two girls who are serving are wearing absolutely no clothes. They are completely naked, except for glitter painted on their faces. It takes me a few seconds to register what I'm seeing, tits and shaved pussy. Lovely bodies. I admire them as she gets me the waters.

As I look around, I start to notice naked people and quite a few are indulging in sex of some kind, whether it be oral or penetrative. I'm shocked and it takes a few seconds for it all to sink in.

I look around to see if anyone else has noticed, but no one is batting an eyelid at this. BGC laugh at my reaction because I assume my face looks a picture of shock.

'I hope you don't mind, Bree, but this is sex club ya.' I don't mind and I tell them this.

'We go sit in the best seat in the house' and I'm led to the stage area where a row of seats can be found at the back of the stage and against the wall.

'We have best view ya,' says BGG and she indicates the dance floor and the bar. She is right, this is the best view in the place.

The night just gets crazier.

Right in front of us, is a swing. Not any old child's swing, no, this is a sex swing which I discover when I see it getting used. The club is full now and everyone has dressed appropriately, with barely a stitch on. Men and men, women and women and women and men, are having sex of some kind in every corner as well as on the dance floor. The swing is currently being used by a naked woman who spreads her legs as she swings into the crowds, allowing anyone near to either finger her or lick her. She is loving it.

I'm being watched for my reaction from BGC and they can tell I'm loving it! Never in my life have I ever seen anything like it. A few people, both men and women, have come up to me to say something but BGC have swatted them away in German.

'What do they want,' I ask the second time it happens.

'To fuck you, Bree,' says BGB.

I'm flattered.

I'm lively, as the pills have kicked in, but I don't want to dance and nor do BGC. They say it is best we stay where we are as we'll lose our seats.

'I need to wee' and BGG takes me to the toilet. We walk through the crowd, and I'm touched, pinched, stroked and kissed as I make my way, but BGG won't let go of my hand so I feel safe.

As we wait to use the toilets, a guy walks up and down the line asking to be pissed on. He finds someone who agrees, and off they go to the men's toilets. I find this hilarious.

'It is good to be pissed on ya,' says BGG, but I can't say I've ever tried it. 'You should, ist fun.'

We make our way through the crowds and avoid the dance floor, which is full of people dancing and fucking and eventually get back to our seats. 'You come back to ours tonight, ya,' says BGB and I look at him quizzically.

'Ya, she likes you to come back and play ya,' as he nods towards BGG, who is smiling at me and stroking my hair and all of a sudden, I get it. She wants to have sex with me and I don't have to think for longer than a second.

'I'd love that,' I say, and with that, we get up off the best seats in the house and head outside to catch a cab to their place, somewhere in Berlin.

37

I've dabbled from time to time with the same sex, but I've never actually had sex with a woman. Still, here I am in the back of a taxi kissing the face off BGG and the feeling is electric.

Her face is soft, as are her lips, and it's sensual and sexy. I have never wanted sex as badly as I want it now. I want to get to her place as soon as possible, I've almost forgotten that BGB is with us too.

We pull up outside a large apartment block somewhere in Berlin, BGB pays the fare whilst me and BGG make our way, hand in hand, up to two flights of stairs where she lets me into a cosy and inviting apartment. She leads me into the lounge and offers to get me a drink.

While she's in the kitchen, I start to skin up a joint for us all to enjoy. BGB comes into the lounge, sits on the recliner, and starts to talk.

'So, you like Berlin, ya?' He doesn't need to ask that question again, he can tell I'm having the time of my life, and it's about to get a lot better.

BGG sits next to me and starts to kiss me again.

'Why don't you go have a shower' offers BGB, and we both giggle with excitement at the thought. It is also very needed. There is no way I'm having sex with anyone without getting the stick of the Kit Kat off me.

We go into her bathroom and undress each other. It's so sensual I don't know whether it's the drugs or if this is how it really feels when you are with a woman, but I love it, and it suddenly dawns on me, am I a lesbian?

Before I can analyse this question, we are in the shower, and she's washing me. She has a sponge, and she starts with my breasts and works her way down until the sponge is between my legs. As she brushes it against me, it feels like electricity coursing through my body. I moan slightly at the pleasure and I know I will orgasm before her tongue has tasted me.

With eyes closed and my body leaning against the wall of the shower, the pleasure comes in waves through my body. She kisses me deeply and turns off the shower, leading me into the lounge, wet, naked and horny for more.

I don't feel any embarrassment that I'm fully naked in front of BGC. I'm just thankful I'm slim and brown. BGB approves of my body by touching me between my legs and asking me if I'm enjoying myself. I nod happily like a child at Christmas.

BGC start to kiss each other, and I sit back on the couch and watch them. He is hard, and he pulls her onto him. She is straddled across him, and he enters her with such force that she yelps in pain.

He is looking over her shoulder at me and indicates for me to start touching myself, which I do. I'm so horny from my live porn show.

She has turned around now and is facing me, allowing me a better view of his cock going into her, and I have never felt so horny in my life. She calls me over and asks me to lick her as he pounds her. I kneel between his legs and start to lick the shaft of his cock. I suck in his balls, and he moans softly in pleasure. This spurs him on to fuck her harder and once I've finished licking his balls, I make my way up to her clit, which is enlarged and swollen. I lick it like I'm licking an ice cream and she grabs my hair and directs me to go faster until I can feel her cum at the same time as he does.

We all pull away breathless from the marathon session we have all had and take time out to have a drink and a spliff and chill.

After a while BGB is now ready for more, and he wants me this time, and I oblige. He does things to me that I've never done before, and I love every minute of it. We continue long into the night and next day and don't stop until it's time for me to go home.

At 6pm I get into the taxi to be taken back to my apartment and I thank them for giving me the best night of my life.

'It's what we do, ya,' he says.

'Danke Bree, come back and see us again when you are next in Berlin,' she says.

And I promise myself that if I ever go back to Berlin, I'll be staying with them for a week.

38

I get to the house at lunchtime, Sam and Jess are home, waiting for me. I've been missed, and I've missed them too. I have no intention of unpacking. I just want to sit in the lounge, smoke weed and tell them about my amazing trip to Berlin.

It takes me over an hour to finish my story. They are enthralled and jealous and want us to book a trip to Berlin as soon as possible.

'AND you'll never guess what I did Friday night at the Kit Kat Klub,' as I proceed to tell them my juiciest story ever.

'I can't believe it,' says Jess.

'So, you're a lesbian now?' asks Sam.

'No, I don't think so, but I am definitely a convert to pussy,' and we laugh at this bit of news.

'We have to go to Kit Kat,' they both say in unison. I agree that we must. No one can believe what goes on there without seeing it with their own eyes.

'What's been happening with you two,' I ask, but I know it will be nothing like my escapades.

'We've been boring darling, not the same without you,' says Sam.

'Hey, thanks, Sam! I thought we had a great weekend last week. I took him to the Redback. You loved it, didn't you, Sam?' says Jess with a laugh.

'What happened?' because I know they have a story to tell.

'He only goes and scores himself a hot boyfriend from the Redback, didn't you?'

And Sam goes into detail about how he hated the place at first, too many breeders for his liking. Still, he'd met Nick, a lovely Canadian guy there who'd been dragged out by his flatmates as well. They had talked for ages and swapped numbers.

They are yet to go on their first date, but Sam is planning on meeting him in Soho this weekend for a drink, and who knows.

'He's scrummy Bree; wait till you meet him,' says Sam, eyes all sparkly.

'He is scrummy and such a waste,' says Jess a little bit enviously.

'And you?' I say to Jess. I'm getting the feeling she has something to tell me.

A look goes between Jess and Sam.

'What?' I say a bit more defensively.

'Okay, I hooked up with someone, but you aren't going to like it.'

And before she opens her mouth, I know what she's going to say.

'It's Juan's mate Jack. Look, Bree, I won't see him if it's weird for you, but he's so gorgeous, and I've wanted him for ages.'

Jess and Jack had made a play for each other when Juan and I first got together, but for some reason or another, it just didn't happen beyond the first night.

'Jess, if he's into you and you're into him, who am I to say no, just because Fucktard got married' the room starts laughing at my new nickname for him (never will I say his name out loud).

'So, have you shagged him yet,' but I know the answer to that too.

She gushes over him, his big cock, great tongue, and interesting conversation, but I switch off when she says he's coming over that evening.

'I'll be sure to go to bed early then.'

'Don't be like that Bree, he really likes you.'

'Yeah, whatever, I really don't want to hear how their honeymoon went.'

'I already know, and it wasn't good, according to Jack,' says Jess. Now I'm interested.

According to Jack, Juan had a shit honeymoon in Ibiza because he wanted to party every night, and she didn't.

'Why pick fucking Ibiza for your honeymoon if you aren't going to party?' were Jack's words.

And he is right, but a feeling of absolute joy comes over me when I hear this news and I feel relieved for some reason. I had imagined them having the best time ever. Sex three times a day, like I know he can, but instead, I hear he was miserable, and I don't feel sorry for him one little bit.

'Does this mean I'm over him?' I ask Sam later.

'Bree, you've been over him since the minute you touched down in Berlin by the sounds of it.'

And I think, yes, maybe I am.

I go to bed early as planned and long before Jack comes over to service Jess. It feels good to be back in my own bed, between my clean Ariel smelling sheets, and I fall asleep dreaming of BGC and wonder if actually I am a lesbian.

39

I've been back from Berlin for 2 weeks now, and I'm still yearning to go back though it has been good getting back into the swing of things in Acton, and Jodie is so much nicer to me now.

We've spoken a couple of times since I got back, and she said she was impressed with my work and if there is a need for me, she'll call me back. I offered to go at any time as I'd had so much fun.

'Yeah, I heard,' she'd said, and I wondered what she was referring too. My drug-taking? My session with BGC? I feel self-conscious but I don't pry as to what she meant. I am too scared to ask.

I didn't tell anyone at work what had happened with BGC and I didn't tell anyone about Jodie taking bucket loads of drugs. She didn't ask me to keep it quiet, I just got the feeling it should be a secret between us, and if I didn't blab my mouth to the others, she might trust me enough to go back.

'I want to work in the Berlin office for 2 weeks,' whines Jonny, but William has told him it isn't an option, and he needs him to stay in the London office.

'He wants you all to himself,' I joke with Jonny, who dismisses my comment with a blush.

'We need to go out and have a work piss up,' I offer to the team. It is still summer. London rocks in the summer and I want to make the most of it before winter sets in.

But disappointingly, no one seems interested in going out. We used to be a mad party team, but things have changed since I got back from Berlin, and I can't quite work it out.

'I'm too busy,' says William.

'I'm way too busy,' says Jonny.

'I don't want to,' says Aggie.

'Ah well, fuck you all, then I'll make my own plans,' I say in a bit of strop. I have Jess and Sam to go out with, but with the two of them all loved up, it can be boring. Sometimes you just need a different group. I long to go back to Berlin where I'd made friends so easily. I'll go next year if Man Source is still open.

I got the impression when I was there that Jodie was ready to go back to Australia. She'd mentioned several times how she was done with Berlin and had made her money. Lucky bitch.

But for now, we are still recruiting for Berlin, and we are super busy. We are mobilising over 40 men a week as there is a push to get the job done. Berlin becomes the capital city of Germany once again, in less than 4 months. The pressure is on to get the city ready for the year 2000.

'The Redback is selling tickets for New Years; we should get them in before they sell out,' I say to the team. There are a few murmurs, but no one wants to commit.

'I'm happy to get them in to make sure we've got somewhere to go; I really don't want to be left out of the party of the year,' I continue.

'Just get the tickets, Bree, to be sure,' says William.

I call Jess at work and ask her what her thoughts are.

'I suppose it's close, and we are guaranteed a good time,' is her response.

I tell the team it's already been agreed that we are going to the Redback for the Millennium New Year party and that someone had to make the decision which I have done.

'Ok, do what you need to do darl and let me know what I owe,' says William.

'So, we're off to the Redback,' says Jonny to Willy.

'Fuck it, just get me 2 tickets,' says Aggie reluctantly.

'Two?' I ask.

'Ya, two,' says Aggie but offers no other explanation. We realise that Aggie and Smokey must be serious if she wants two tickets, four months out from New Year.

40

Aggie doesn't remember exactly when she fell in love with Smokey, but she remembers when she first said the words.

Smokey had already told her she was in love a few weeks before. She'd broken up with her boyfriend at the time and had made a commitment to Aggie.

Aggie was nervous about falling in love and committing to her. She'd been in this position a few times with a straight woman and it never worked out. They always went back to cock. Why would Smokey be any different?

But Smokey had persisted. They had been away on romantic weekends to the Cotswolds and most recently, Scotland, and the time they had spent together had been the most amazing. In fact, Aggie believed these last few months had been the best in her life. Smokey had said the same. She couldn't believe how perfect their relationship was and how she had never entertained the idea of falling in love with a woman. Still, here she was, a few months in, telling this beautiful German woman how much she loved her.

Aggie wasn't ready to say the words out loud when Smokey had declared her love, yet right now, while they are lying in bed after yet another amazing sex session, she felt ready.

They are lying back in Aggie's bed, smoking a joint and stroking each other as they lay back against the pillows and the feeling comes over her in a wave.

'I love you,' says Aggie.

'I know,' says Smokey.

The feeling is overwhelming for them both and they shed a tear in a moment of pure love.

'I want you forever, you know that right,' says Smokey.

'Forever is long, babe, but ya, I want you forever too.'

'I think a visit to my family soon ya, maybe in the new year.'

'And we must go to Israel and meet mine.'

Smokey had been worried her family wouldn't accept her being with a woman, but when she'd told her mum over the phone, she'd been surprised at her response.

'As long as my daughter is happy, we will be happy,' she'd said.

Aggies family have known since she was a teenager that she is gay, so Aggie didn't have to come out. She just let them know she'd met someone special, and she was happy.

They excitedly start making plans for next year now that they can both see a future together.

'But first, I must make love to you again,' says Aggie, and Smokey doesn't say no, to the best sex she has ever had.

41

For the last few weeks, I've been quiet as far as socialising is concerned. I've even managed to go two weeks off any Class A's, and I've been feeling fabulous. However, I'm bored out of my mind, I need to party, and I'm due to be laid as well. I haven't had sex since BGC and I'm beginning to have sex dreams. These dreams come to me nightly. They usually consist of me having sex with someone revolting, like the corner shop man, or worse, William (I had a dream last night that he and I had sex, yuk).

When I start getting the dreams, my body is telling me it's time to get laid, so I'm thinking we need a session at the Redback so that a. I can take drugs and b. I can meet someone for a random one night.

No one from Man Source is interested in a Saturday night session at the Reddy, so I convince Sam and Jess to come with me.

'Why don't we start at the Walkabout in Shepherds Bush Saturday afternoon and make our way to the Reddy later?' I suggest.

'Great idea, babe, and let's get the goodies arranged too,' Sam is referring to coke.

I call Pablo at 10am, hoping I don't wake him, but he's already up and delivering and promises to pop in before we are due to leave at 12 noon.

He comes when he's supposed to, stays for a cup of tea, and leaves us to get ready for a Saturday session. I'm excited. It feels like forever since we did this.

Autumn has set in well and truly, so I'm not wearing my little skirts and crop tops anymore. Jeans and a low plunging top will do, as well as a jacket for when it rains, which it will because this is London and its Autumn.

We get to the Walkie in good time as it's close to our house and the place is already filling up. The Australasian pubs in London seem to get a bit quieter as we head into winter. I can only assume most backpackers prefer to be home and in the sunshine, than here in dreary London. Don't get me wrong, there are still shit loads of them here but not as many as summer; well, that's how it feels to me.

We get served, find a table with a view of the dance floor and we start to drink. Coke always gives me the ability to down pint after pint without feeling the effects of the alcohol. A bit dangerous, really, but I don't worry about such things at my age.

247

'I'm in the mood to get laid,' I say wickedly to my gang, and they laugh and tell me to go for it.

'I hope you don't mind, but Jack is meeting up with us later,' says Jess. I'm disappointed but don't show it. Just lately, it's all been about Jack, and I haven't been hanging out with Jess because of it. I find it too close for comfort, knowing he speaks to Fucktard on the daily.

'Yes, my man will be joining us too,' says Sam. He has also been neglecting me for Nick, and I'm feeling left out.

'Well, that does it. I'm going to have to find myself a boyfriend with you two carrying on as if you're about to get married' I say this jokingly, but I'm half serious too.

'As if' they both screech in unison, and my mind is put at ease, for now.

We decide to make our way to Acton High Street by bus and jump on the 207 that takes us all the way up the Uxbridge Road and delivers us opposite the Redback.

We can see a line has started to form, but we don't care; we are in no rush. We've had a good afternoon at the Walkie and its now time to dance off the last of our energy at the Reddy.

We'd been checking out the talent at the Walkie, but no one caught my eye. I have faith in the Redback Tavern as 99% of the time, it hasn't let me down.

The familiar smell of the place hits us as we eventually walk through the front doors, and the place is heaving! The toilet line is long, as is the queue at the bar, and we decide we've had enough to drink and just want to dance.

The usual Aussie rock is playing, and we are in the mood for a bit of headbanging, knocking into people, and having a jolly old time. Through the next song, I notice Jack making his way through the crowd and over to our group.

He gives Jess a passionate kiss and starts to sway with us. He tries to say something to me, but it's too noisy and I'm not bothered by what he says. I'm too busy rubbing myself up against the hunk behind me, who for the last 2 songs had been rubbing his cock against my arse.

'Bree, Juan is here with Charlene,' Jess shouts in my ear and in that instant, my light mood turns dark, and I look wildly around to see if he can see me. I can't see them and decide my night is now over and I want to go home.

'Ah, don't be like that Bree, you're gonna have to get used to bumping into him, hey,' says Sam. But I'm not ready to see the happy couple and their sparkling wedding rings.

'Nah, Sam, I'm ready to call it a night, babe, don't worry about me. I'm good, I want to go home.'

They kiss me goodbye and carry on dancing. I look back at the Hunk who'd been rubbing his cock against me, but he's already rubbing himself up against someone else. So, my potential shag for the night has made other plans. Fine by me, I just want to get out of here before I see them.

As I pull myself from the dance floor and head towards the door, I see her, Bitchface, looking healthy and happy, smiling out at the crowd. Then I see it, for all its glory. Her pregnant belly protruding through her maternity top, and in that split second, I work out she must be 6 months pregnant, at least!

It stops me in my tracks and a lump forms in my throat as I watch her swaying slightly to the music, a lemonade in her hand. He is standing next to her, and his eyes are searching the crowd. Something makes him look over and we make eye contact. He must have seen the pain on my face because his eyes crinkle in a sad, I'm sorry way. It takes all my will power not to storm over there, slap his face and let her know he was shagging me when she was pregnant, but I don't. She's now seen who he is looking at, and she slaps his arm, which breaks the spell between us. I turn around and storm out of the door, onto the wet, cold, dark street.

I stomp down the road like a raging bull, and if anyone has an idea to mug or rape me, they stay away. I am a scorned woman with steam pouring out of my ears, and I do this the whole journey home.

Not until I open my front door and slam it behind me, do I let out the wail of utter misery that has been building up inside me for the 20-minute walk home.

I lean my back against the front door, knees up to my face and sob tears of pity and grief, not stopping until the tears run dry. At some stage that night, I eventually make my way to my bedroom, get undressed and roll a spliff. As I lay there smoking and thinking, but not crying, I swear to the universe, to God, to my unborn children that I will never ever cry another tear over him, until the day I die.

42

'I wanted to tell you, babe, I just didn't want to ruin your happiness as you've been great since getting back from Berlin,' says Jess the next morning, once she knows that I know about Charlene.

I can't even call her Bitchface anymore because she's pregnant and it doesn't seem right.

My eyes are puffy from last night's crying, but I don't tell Jess, Jack, and Sam about my pity party. They can guess that shit just by looking at me.

Jess has been apologising all morning because she knows I know that Jack would have told her.

'What hurts Jess is that she has been pregnant for some time and I was shagging him when he would have known he was going to be a dad.'

'That's why the wedding was brought forward because her parents did not want her to have a baby out of wedlock,' Jack offered as an explanation.

I don't like Jack. He is Juan's good friend, and I don't trust him. Hence, why I'm not bawling my eyes out and being a pathetic loser in love. He'd report that shit straight back, I'm sure.

'You should thank your lucky stars it's not you knocked up by the twat,' says Sam helpfully.

'Yeah, exactly,' says Jess. But I don't feel lucky. I feel stupid.

'I'm tired of talking about him and I wish *her* the best of luck. She is going to need it, and, at the end of the day, there is now going to be a baby involved. It's time to put this to bed and not mention it again, please,' I implore the room.

'Today is Sunday; we only have a few weeks left before Christmas. I think we should go to the pub for lunch and plan our parties,' I say with as much joy in my voice as I can muster.

Jess knows me well and knows I'm hurting badly inside, but because of Jack, I can't show it, which is a good thing.

'Which pub?' asks Jess.

'How about we try The Raven at Stamford Brook,' Sam suggests. He has been hanging out there quite a bit with his new man and the food is meant to be awesome.

After a morning of doing nothing other than sitting in the lounge, drinking coffee, and smoking spliff, we get ready and head out to the underground for the short trip to Stamford Brook. The pub is opposite the station, and so it's an easy and quick journey. The atmosphere in the pub is perfect for a wintery Sunday afternoon.

We find a table, each orders the Roast of the Day and a few pints of cider and we spend the afternoon doing what 20 something-year-old's do in London in the '90s.

Nobody mentions Juan and his impending fatherhood, and though I feel empty inside, I also know I will never shed another tear over him.

That night as I'm getting ready for bed and dreading Monday morning in the office, Jess comes to see me for a chat. It's been a while since we didn't have Jack here taking up her time, and it's nice to smoke spliffs and giggle like we used to.

'You'll be ok Bree, you're made of tough stuff, babe.'

'I know.'

'Shall we have a Halloween party to cheer us all up?' says Jess.
'I'd love that, babe, leave it with me. I'll start the planning.'

43

I've been madly planning yet another Party of the Decade, and this time the theme is Halloween.

The usual crew have been invited and a few new friends that we've met along the way. Sam and Nick are going strong, and I do believe they are in love.

Jess and Jack are still in the honeymoon period of their relationship, and it's nice to see her so happy and in love. Jack has grown on me these last few weeks, and though he doesn't mention them very often, the bits of information he has shared has always been in a negative light.

Things like 'she's a moody bitch' or 'I know he gets it less than he ever did' cheers me up and I feel lucky I escaped when I did. Me, I've been plodding along alone, for the first time in a long time, and it feels good to not need or want to be with a man, or woman for that matter. I think of BGC often and plan to get to Berlin in the new year.

The usual goodies have been ordered for Saturday night. Fifty ecstasy pills (one for every guest), 4 grams of coke (my own stash, everyone else can fuck off and buy their own), a ton of alcohol and the theme is dress up. My favourite kind of party.

We decorate the house in spooky-themed decoration. Lots of spider web fluff has been strewn all over the lounge and front door, making it clear to anyone who walks past that this house on Antrobus Road is about to have a mega Halloween party. We've invited the neighbours to keep them happy, knowing they won't attend and hoping they've planned a night away. If they are clever, they will do this. Our parties are loud and go on for a long time.

Pablo shows his face early to deliver the goodies and says he wants to attend this one for some reason. He never really stays anywhere and I just figure the man needs to party sometimes too. His hours are very antisocial and he's always making the party good, yet never getting the benefit from it. I wonder if it is Pablo I will end up in bed with tonight because even though I'm loving being alone and single, I'm still horny and need a man between my legs.

The party starts off early, and by 10pm, the house is full. Aggie and Smokey are the first to arrive, and they decline my generous offer of a pill. They are dressed as the sexiest witches I've ever seen.

'Ve don't need that tonight' had been Aggie's explanation about taking ecstasy. They are such a cute couple, and they make out in the corner of the lounge for most of the night before leaving early. I was aware they had gone and I vaguely remember them coming up to me and giving me a kiss goodbye, but I wasn't paying them too much attention.

Jonny and William had rocked up together quite late and were happy to take a pill. 'You throw an awesome party, bru' is Johnny's way of telling me he is having fun.

'Yes, darl, I love your parties,' says William. They both mingle with the rest of the guests, and at one stage, I think I remember them dancing to some mad tune I had put on.

They haven't bothered getting dressed for my party, but I am ok with this, all I wanted was for them to attend, which they have.

Most people who attend are dressed the part. There are scary clowns, zombies and a lot of witches and wizards. Pablo arrives late, and he looks exhausted. I ask him if he wants a line or pill, but he declines. I suppose he can't really take the drugs if he's to sell them. Being a drug dealer would not work for me at all. I have tried it once, but I was high on my own supply, and people still owe me. Not the career I need to follow.

We speak for a while, but I am keen to get back onto the dance floor, aka lounge and show off my newly learnt Berlin dance moves. The soundtrack is pure trance. It is the right music for the drugs we are all on.

The party starts to wind down at around 2am, which is early for us. I notice that Sam and Jess have already gone to bed with their respective partners. I'm here alone in the kitchen smoking a spliff, and I'm not feeling ready for bed.

I look around the kitchen, and it's a mess, but right now, I don't want to worry about it. I was surprised that Pablo left when he did because I was going to make a move. He probably wasn't interested in me with my big wide eyes and random chat, and I don't think being with someone straight tonight would be a good thing.

As I make my way to the stairs, planning on trying to sleep, I see a reflection at the front door of someone trying to get in, so I rush over to answer it, hoping it is someone from the party who wants to carry on, but as I open the door, there in front of me is Juan, the Fucktard. He looks handsome and he is wearing a smile that just makes his face shine. It's probably the drink and drugs, but man he looks hot.

I'm so shocked I don't say a word and I can't help myself as I move towards him and start kissing him. I jump on him, legs wrapped around his waist and I let him carry me upstairs and into my bedroom.

He throws me onto the bed and starts to pull my jeans and knickers off in one move. He barely gets his jeans to his ankles before he is entering me and fucks me harder than I've ever been fucked before and it is fabulous and exactly what I want. He pins my hands down beside my face and kisses me passionately and deeply with such urgency I know he isn't going to last long.

Usually, after he's cum, he falls asleep. Not tonight. The sex continues into the early hours of the morning before he needs to rest and sit back and smoke spliff.

We haven't said a word to each other except things like 'fuck me harder' or 'keep doing that I'm going to cum,' and the conversation does not start even now.

We finish our smoke, still not saying a word and then I notice he is falling asleep, but by now I'm sobering up and coming down,

I've had my fill of cock, and I don't want him in my bed anymore.

'Hey, you can't sleep Juan, I need you gone,' I say. The shock on his face is fleeting, and then he smiles that smile.

'Bree, come on babe, you're not still mad hey, let me sleep a bit longer, and you might just get it again.'

'No mate, I need you out of my bed now please, I've had what I need and I want to be alone today,' I insist.

He thinks I'm joking for a few seconds, but then he realises the power is back in my court, and I don't want him anymore. I used him as much as he used me, and I want him gone.

'For fuck sake, Bree, stop your crazy shit yeah, no wonder we broke up.'

'You are such a dickhead, now get out of my bed and out of my house and don't ever come back. Go back to your wife, you fucking idiot,' and I say this through gritted teeth but with a smile on my face.

He can see he's entered the danger zone and says nothing more. He gets up out of bed, gets dressed and walks out of my bedroom. I can hear the front door slam shut a few seconds later. He shuts it so hard the windows rattle, and the satisfaction of knowing he's pissed off and feeling used, makes my year; no, it actually makes my life!

44

Juan can recall the exact moment he realised he'd made a mistake proposing to Charlene, and that was the day she had excitedly told him she was pregnant and they needed to bring the wedding forward.

When he'd proposed to her, he had been off his chops on ecstasy, as was she. He thought life couldn't get better, and he wanted this woman forever. She'd also been making massive hints since moving in with him that he would have to make an honest woman of her if he wanted this to continue.

When he had woken from his drugged-up state and realised he'd proposed, he figured he would stall the wedding date by a few years. Charlene had wasted no time telling her family and everyone that knew her, and that's when she hounded him to set a date. He tried to change the subject every time she mentioned it, but Charlene knew he was stalling and wasn't quite into getting married. She hatched her plan, and she got what she wanted, the pregnancy.

Just a few months after meeting her, he had a wedding date booked and a baby on the way. It made him feel sick just thinking about it, and the feeling of being trapped would not leave his thoughts. He acted happy and excited, but deep down, he was terrified he'd made the biggest mistake of his life. He knows he loves Charlene, but it isn't the intense love he had felt at the beginning when he couldn't get enough of her. He reflects now that Bree hadn't really been that pushy, only wanting to travel with him, and he is wishing he hadn't been so hasty in getting rid of her.

When Bree had texted to say she was having a party and he was invited, he knew he'd be going and told Charlene he was going out with his mates. Charlene had started to 'nest' and wasn't interested in going out anymore. She couldn't take drugs or drink, and the sex was beginning to dry up too, in case they hurt the baby. He was feeling miserable. He was even more miserable when he'd turned up at Bree's party, only to be told she was upstairs shagging her flatmate. He'd gone home in a foul mood and had had his first massive fight with Charlene, which ended up with her sobbing and threatening to leave for South Africa and taking their unborn baby with her. He was gutted and apologised and begged Charlene to stay. He really felt his life was falling apart but, at the same time, couldn't get Bree out of his head.

And he had won Bree back, slowly but surely, not committing to anything, just keeping her where he wanted her, at his beck and call when Charlene said no to his sexual demands. Bree always came through with the goods. Desperate, pathetic Bree.

But Bree wasn't so desperate and pathetic, and before he knew what had happened, she had used him for one last fuck and had thrown him out of her house. And he had realised at that moment that he quite liked Bree and that he had fucked it up so badly, he was never going to get her back.

And now here he is, married to Charlene and a baby on the way, all within 12 months of meeting her, and he curses the day he laid eyes on her tits and let his cock rule his head.

45

The team could not believe it when I told them what had happened on Saturday night. I got a lot of praise for my courage, and Aggie loved the fact I had fucked him and thrown him out of my bed when I'd finished.

'Das ist gut Bree' she had said encouragingly.

'You have closure, darl,' says William.

'You go, my china,' says Jonny.

And I'm so happy. Hungover and hanging still from Saturday night on the pills, but I'm happy, and yes, I have closure.

Things have really slowed down in Berlin, which means the Acton office is also quiet, and so we are all quite bored and smoking a lot out in the courtyard.

William is distracted this morning, and he keeps looking at the door as if he's expecting someone important to come through, and around 10am, she does. Jodie.

When I see her face, I know why she is here, and my stomach drops with nerves. I don't want to lose my job, but at this time of year, and with no more new contracts being signed by Man Source, I knew our time was numbered. I just wasn't expecting it so close to Xmas. I mentally make a note of all the savings I have, and it's not much. A month or two, and I'll have nothing. Getting another job at this time of the year will also prove hard, and tears spring to my eyes with the worry.

I can see from everyone's faces that they are all thinking the same. There is an air of anticipation, and we wait to see what must be said.

After doing the rounds of hellos and how are you doing, Jodie comes to stand in the middle of the office, with her back to the kitchen so she can face us all and asks Aggie to lock the front door as she has an announcement.

'I just want to start by saying thank you to you all for an amazing year. Without you here in London, I would not have been able to fulfil my contracts and exceed some of them. Our reputation in the industry is second to none, and that's because of all your efforts and hard work over the last few months.'

I try not to laugh out loud at the 'all of our hard work' comment. I don't remember any of us working hard this year; we've partied hard, though. She continues.

'So, on that note, it makes this harder for me right now because, after lots of discussions with William and my backers in Berlin, I've come to the decision to wind Man Source down with our last day being this Friday.'

I burst into tears at the news as I wasn't expecting it to be so soon. Jonny comes over and gives me a hug.

'Don't cry Bree, everything will be ok,' offers Jodie as reassurance, but I don't feel reassured at all. We are 6 weeks from Xmas and the biggest party of the Millennium, and we are all being laid off on Friday.

'As a thank you to all of you for your hard work, I will be paying bonuses, and you will be paid out a month's notice, so I'm hoping this will ease your pain of not working over this time.' This news is music to our ears, and we start to smile again.

'And Friday I want to take you all for a goodbye lunch so the office will be officially closed from 12noon.'

This must have been planned for weeks. I know William must have known, and I'm hurt he didn't warn us. As if he has read my mind, he indicates we go out the back to die, and I follow him for what is one of the last times we'll ever do this, and I feel like crying again.

'Don't worry Bree, your bonus is going to be a good one. You'll need to think wisely about what you want to do with it?' he says as we puff on our Marlboro Lights.

'Like, how significant are we talking,' I ask hopefully.

'Let's just say it's going to be a few thousand pounds. I can't say exactly how much because I don't know, but Friday we'll find out.'

'Why didn't you tell us,' I ask accusingly.

'Darl, if you had known this information before she said anything, she'd have had my guts for garters, and I'm not in the mood to be told off by Jodie.'

We wander back into the office. Jodie has been talking to Aggie and Jonny, and they are laughing at something she has said. I'm jealous I've missed it.

Jodie tells us that she and William are going out for the day as they have lots to do before Friday. We know we won't see the pair of them for a few days, and that's ok with us.

To my surprise, William is back in the office the next day and for the rest of the week, and I ask him why he isn't partying hard with Jodie. Still, he doesn't say much except she's not feeling her best, and this week isn't the week for parties.

He's distracted and grumpy, and we put it down to us all losing our jobs, but by Friday, he's back to his usual sarcastic self.

Jodie seems relieved that we've got to the last day, and she can finally say goodbye to her brainchild that has made her millions and kept her busy for the best part of three years.

As we walk out of the office and turn off the lights for the last time, I'm sad and nostalgic and know I'm going to miss this place more than I can ever imagine. I am crying quietly as I watch William lock the front door for the last time. The team look as sad as me, and I'm sure William is crying too.

Me, Aggie, and Jonny link arms as we walk along the High Street towards The George pub a bit further up the road, and we don't care that people have to walk around us. It takes less than 10 minutes to get there, we order lunch, though none of us are hungry, and a round of drinks.

Much to my surprise, Jodie informs me she's given up smoking and isn't drinking right now as she's on a health kick. I'm shocked. A few months ago, she took drugs by the bucket load and chain-smoked 40 a day.

'Wow, what made you decide to get healthy?' I ask in surprise.

'It has to happen at some stage, and now is a good time. The end of Berlin, London and maybe a trip home to Australia,' she muses but ends the conversation by turning to Jonny and talking to him.

We eat our lunch when it arrives and when we are all on our second drinks, Jodie decides it's time for the final team meeting. This is the bit we are waiting for; we are all dying to know what our bonus is going to be.

Aggie thinks we'll get a few thousand. Jonny has predicted £500. I will be happy with anything right now as my bank balance will not support me for long.

We'd been talking all week about what we are all going to do and where we are going after Man Source.

Jonny was vague but had mentioned staying in London to find another recruitment role in the city now that he has experience. Aggie and Smokey will travel to Germany and Israel and see where they land after that. William isn't sure. He has talked about staying in London for a while with a trip back to Sydney. Me, I have no idea. I suppose I will need a job and will start looking again in January when Christmas and New Year is over. I like the idea of travelling somewhere warm for winter, but that will depend on the bonus.

'Ok, this is a sad day for me. Man Source has been my baby for 3 years and has been the best and worst thing I have ever done. The highs outweighed the lows, and there's been a few of those' she looks at William when she says this. 'It wasn't an easy decision, but with Berlin almost complete and the contracts getting smaller and smaller, I'd rather leave on a high, with the memories and the knowledge that we were part of this monumental event in history.'

I look around and can see that we are all perched on the edge of seats, waiting for her to finish with her emotional speech and take us straight to the money. She must have felt the vibe because she reaches into her bag and pulls out three white envelops. Each one has our names on it. Bree. Jonny. Aggie.

271

'I'm not going to go on too much longer because I have so much to do, but I want to give you all a little something to help you get through the next weeks and to show you how thankful I am for all your hard work.'

She hands them out to us all and waits for us to look inside. In each envelope, there are 20 x 1000DM notes, which works out to be approximately £10,000 each. We sit there with our mouths open in happy shock, and it takes a few seconds before we are jumping up from our seats, hugging Jodie, and thanking her. We hug each other and William even leans in for one too.

'William has his own envelope before you ask,' says Jodie, but we'd guessed he'd got his envelope already, and I'm sure it was much larger than ours. We are so happy with the bonus and in complete shock at how much we got. Never in my wildest dreams did I imagine we'd get this much, and it changes everything because now I have enough money to go anywhere in the world.

Jodie and William do not stay for long, and after a few minutes of more small talk and lots of thank you for the money from us, they make their excuses and leave us in the pub to marvel at our good luck.

'Don't go partying with that money in your pockets, ok; take it to the bank now' was Jodie's advice before leaving, and we all agree that is exactly what we are going to do before going home. We order a couple more pints, but Jonny wants to go home and has been quiet for most of the conversation.

'Are you ok?' I ask, concerned. He's not his perky self lately and I wonder what is going on in his life. In fact, the more I think about it, the more I've come to realise that he's been quiet for a while now. No stories of his love life or breaking his cock on some bird he'd pulled.

'Ya china, I'm fine, I have lots to think about, but I'll call you and let's arrange to hang out soon, ok?'

I give Jonny and Aggie a kiss on the cheek goodbye, and we hug a little bit longer than normal, knowing we are never going to work together again.

I pop into Barclay's Bank on my way home and deposit the money once it has been converted. I have never had that much money in my account and I'm itching to go shopping, but today isn't that day. I have plans to make.

That night, sitting with Jess and Sam, who are both so happy for me and a wee bit envious, I tell them my plans. I want to go travelling somewhere warm for a few weeks and did any of them want to come.

'I might be able to come for a couple of weeks,' says Jess.

'I'll come if I can bring my stud muffin,' says Sam.

'I'm thinking Thailand,' I say after a few puffs of my spliff and a sudden urge to go there.

'Yeah, why not,' they say together.

And I do believe that this plan might actually happen, as opposed to all the other crazy ideas we've come up with whilst stoned.

46

It's been just over a week now since we stopped working at Man Source, and I've done nothing except smoke spliff, snort coke and lounge about the house doing nothing.

I've cleaned the house every day, made dinner for my housemates on their return from work, and they both agree they are loving the housewife I've turned into. I know I can't do this forever because I'd go batshit crazy from boredom, but for now, it suits me. We have a massive night planned at The Redback for New Year's Eve, and we also have Christmas Day to get through.

I've arranged to spend it at mum and dads. Jess and Sam are also off to their respective families. We intend to come back on Boxing Day and party hard, because we'll need it by then.

Jonny has called me a couple of times, and Aggie has texted me. We are meeting up at The Spotted Dog in Willesden this Saturday night for a catch-up, and I'm so looking forward to seeing the crew from Man Source.

William has been silent and is yet to respond to my text asking if he's ok. According to Jonny, he's been busy making plans for his future, so I know he's been communicating with at least one of us. As for Jodie, I've heard nothing from her, so I intend to send her an email at some stage to wish her all the best for her next adventures.

I arrange for Pablo to sort me out some coke for Saturday night and I wait excitedly for the night to come. It is miserable and cold out on London's streets and I fancy a session somewhere different from my neck of the woods. Willesden is just far enough for me.

I arrange to meet Aggie on the journey to Willesden. We meet at Hammersmith underground and make our way up north to The Dog. We are both wrapped up in our thickest winter coats, and I'm surprised Smokey isn't joining us.

'She didn't want to,' says Aggie.

We talk about how we've been keeping busy over the last few days and how lucky we still feel. Before we know it, we are at Willesden Green station and ready to walk the 10 minutes to the pub.

The place is busy, the atmosphere feels festive and we find Jonny sitting at the back bar, against the window, with a pint in front of him and a cigarette in his hand. He smiles when he sees us and waves us over to the seats he's been saving. We kiss and hug as if we haven't seen each other in years and he offers to get us both a drink.

While we are waiting for him to get served, I see William walking out of the toilets and over to us. We do another round of hugs and kisses and start to question him about what he's been up to.

'I've been busy, darl, making future plans with all my money,' he winks.

'You have to tell me how much you got; come on, mate, you know what we got,' I beg.

But William is not going to share that information because it's private. Whatever.

'So, what big plans are you making then? Whatever they are, please hire me back,' I say jokingly. He laughs hard at that and I'm not sure if that's a laugh that says, 'no way.'

Jonny eventually gets back with our drinks, and I excuse myself as I need to powder my nose. Again, they all make a collective sniff to indicate that's all I do. Bastards are right, though.

When I get back, they are all grinning at me and I know I've missed something important. I want to know the gossip.

'So, what have I missed? What's the gossip?'

'They have news ya,' says Aggie as she motions towards the boys who are sitting together.

'What?' I ask again.

And with that, William turns to Jonny, kisses him lightly on the lips while looking into his eyes, making sure he is discreet but not discreet enough for me not to understand what is going on.

'Bree, we've something to tell you but don't laugh or take the piss, ok,' says William quite seriously.

'Jonny and I have been seeing each other for a while, and we wanted you both to know.'

It takes a few seconds to register, and then I start laughing at the way they are trying to pull my leg.

'Hey sunshine, it's true, and I'm still trying to come to terms with it' says Jonny just as seriously.

'I'd kiss him if I didn't think I'd get beaten up,' says William.

'They are speaking the truth,' says Aggie.

'And there is more' says Jonny.

How can there be more my brain is screaming? The hunkiest, most straight, most pussy loving guy I've ever met has just told me he's in a relationship with a man.

'So, you're gay now?' I say to Jonny quite scornfully.

'Well, I'd say bi,' says Jonny with a twinkle in his eye, William hits him in the arm, but they are laughing.

I start to laugh too because at that moment I believe them.

'Well, tonight is about celebrating you coming out of the closet, Jonny,' I say, and we all agree to drink to that.

'I told you he was,' says William, and it's true because William has been saying it the whole time.

'Wow, Jonny, now I'll never get to shag you,' I tease but realise that these are not the jokes you tell in front of his possessive and insecure boyfriend.

'So, what else do you have to tell me then? Didn't you say there was something else?'

'I'm also going to be a father,' says Jonny. This time I know he's lying and I snort my drink out all over the table at the joke.

'When are you due, Willian?' I ask mockingly.

But it isn't William who is pregnant, of course. It's Jodie, and this time I really do choke on my drink.

Jonny and William start to tell the story and I'm in shock that I missed it all. Jonny and Jodie had hooked up on one of her secret trips back to London, just after my stay in Berlin, and they had shagged. She'd got pregnant that weekend.

Jonny has only found out recently that she is expecting his baby and wants to keep it. On the other hand, he had to break the news to her that he had come out and was in love with William. Jodie must now process the fact her baby daddy is gay. Still, after a lot of thought, Jodie has decided she'd rather have the help of the gay dad than be a single mum. They have come to an arrangement to co-parent once the baby has arrived. There are no plans for now; they are all trying to come to terms with what has happened over the last few weeks.

'So, you're gay and you're gonna be a dad. Fuck me where have I been through all of this?' is all I can offer, but I'm pleased for them all and it now makes sense that Jodie is on a health kick. She must!

We have a great night together at The Spotted Dog and eventually move on to G.A.Y. in the city for a dance.

I'm still in shock and cannot believe what has happened and nor can Jess when she hears the news, but we wish them all the best, and they've promised to show their faces at The Redback on New Year's.

47

Jodie wanted to get out of Berlin for a weekend and had decided on London, but she didn't want to party with William for once. She knows how hard they both go when they get together, and her body just couldn't take another session. The last time she'd caught up with him, she'd got flu, and it had taken 2 weeks before she had felt herself.

But she needed to get out of Berlin. Since the Love Parade, Jodie had started to take drugs daily. She had been here many times before, and she knows how hard it is to stop. A quiet weekend in London, doing some shopping and eating good food is what she is craving, so she books a room at the Marriot Hotel at Marble Arch, which is close to Bond Street and all the shops she intends to go to.

Jodie doesn't let William know she is in London. She slips through Heathrow and into a cab on Friday morning, having got the early flight out of Tegal. She has paid extra for early check-in and is in her room and unpacked by lunchtime. Once she's had a shower and dressed for a balmy August day in the city, she heads off to Bond Street for some retail therapy. Jodie isn't looking for anything, but as she's the wealthiest she's ever been, and I mean wealthy (think millions), Jodie knows she can shop anywhere she wants and can buy anything she wants.

She spends the day walking up and down Oxford and Regents Street, and by 5pm and £4,000 later, she is ready for a meal, a glass of wine and her bed. She finds herself at Tottenham Court Road and makes her way into Break for the Border for dinner. The place is quiet. She is taken to one of their booths and handed a menu. She picks surf and turf for her main meal and asks for a bottle of Chardonnay. Whilst eating her meal, the place starts to fill up and she decides she'll finish her bottle of wine before catching a cab back to her hotel.

'Hey Jodie, what are you doing here?' She looks up and there is Jonny from the Acton office standing at her table. Fuck. Of all the places he could have picked in the whole of London, he picks here.

'Um, hi Jonny, how are you?' she asks reluctantly, not really caring what his response is. Though he is gorgeous and she'd love to fuck him at some stage, tonight wasn't the planned night. She wanted to be in London anonymously, and now William and the crew will know she was here.

'I'm well, Jodie, just having a birthday meal for one of my flatmates. Hey, what a small world, why don't you come and join us,' says Jonny.

She looks over at the table he is pointing to and sees a small group of men and women. The birthday girl is obvious with her 'it's my birthday' hat on.

'Thanks Jonny; I might join you for a drink later; I just want to finish my wine.'

'Ok, be sure to come and join us before you go,' he says politely, and walks back to his table.

He is obviously talking about her because the table looks over at her as he's speaking. She waves at them. Jodie thinks about calling William to pre-empt the fact he'll be finding out Monday that she was in town, and he will be pissed off she didn't call but decides not to. She'll deal with William once she's back in Berlin.

Jodie continues to drink her wine as the place starts to fill up, and after the bottle has been drunk, she decides that she's not ready to go back to the hotel and will order a cocktail. Once it has arrived and she's paid her bill, she walks over to Jonny's table and sits down next to him.

After all the introductions, a round of tequila shots is delivered and Jodie finds herself shooting one back, just to be polite, of course. It gets a bit awkward for her when their meals arrive and she tells Jonny she is going to go back to the hotel, but he insists she stays.

'Willy didn't tell us you were in town,' he says.

'Yeah nah, I'm having a Willy free weekend, and I'd appreciate it if you don't tell him. He'll get all bitchy if he finds out I didn't invite him.' Jonny assures her that her secret is safe with him.

Once the meals have been cleared away, the serious drinking starts. And man, can this crew drink. What was supposed to be a quiet night in her hotel turns out to be a crazy night on the dance floor.

At some stage, Jonny offers Jodie a line of coke and she happily accepts his offer. They make their way to the men's toilets and lock themselves into a cubicle. Jonny cuts them both two thick lines of some of the finest coke he's ever had, and each take their turn snorting it.

Once it's up their noses, Jodie pushes Jonny against the wall and starts to kiss him frantically and passionately, and they stay face to face for some time until there is an urgent knocking at the door as someone has been waiting for ages to use the toilet.

They come out onto the dance floor and continue to pash. The rest of Jonny's crew are dancing wildly and ordering shots from the Tequila Girl. Jonny and Jodie join in and carry on dancing with the crew.

When it is time to go home, Jodie has other ideas and asks Jonny if he'd like to come back to her hotel. He doesn't say no. They take the short cab ride back to the Marriott and continue their party back at her room.

After taking a shower together, she pops the cork of a bottle of Moet she has ordered through room service and they lie on the bed, both naked, drinking from the bottle.

'Taste me,' says Jodie as she pours champagne over her pussy, and Jonny goes down and starts to lap at her pussy as if he's a dog that hasn't had water for a week. She grabs his hair with both hands, directs his face to her hole and tells him to lick her deeply. Then she brings his face back up to her clit and tells him to lick her slowly. She keeps his face against her pussy for as long as it takes for her to cum and when she does, she screams out in ecstasy whilst grinding herself against him.

While the orgasm is pulsing through her body, he comes up to face her and enters her roughly and deeply, making her cry out in pain and pleasure. He fucks her slowly and deeply and gets into a rhythm that they both enjoy. He doesn't want to cum just yet, so he changes positions and takes her from behind. She's got a nice arse, and he watches as he slaps himself against it while leaning over and grabbing her tits.

He pulls out and forces her face down to his cock and moves her head up and down while she takes it deeply in her mouth, gagging when it goes too deep. He starts to pound her mouth and she can feel he is going to cum, so she stops sucking it, jumps onto it and starts to ride him while on top. It doesn't take long before he's pushing her down deeper onto his cock while he cums inside of her.

They continue to have sex all night while drinking Champagne and snorting his coke. She wanted the coke licked off her clit, and he does as he's told. Between them, they cum multiple times. At some stage in the night, they both fall asleep, and when they wake, they have morning sex. Nothing is awkward between them as they had an amazing night together.

He leaves around 2pm that day, thanking her for an amazing night and promising not to say a word to anyone. Jodie is impressed with Jonny and tells him they'll be hooking up again the next time she's in town. He leaves her with a smile on his face.

Six weeks later, while in Berlin and getting ready to start her day in the office, Jodie wakes up feeling seriously ill and only just makes it to the toilet before throwing up. She's nervous because her period is late, and she's never late. She's been putting off doing the test, but deep down, she knows.

She usually uses condoms, but she hadn't with Jonny, and now here she was at the chemist buying a 2 pack Instant Result Pregnancy Test. She goes into the office toilet and pisses on the stick. Two minutes later, there are the two bright pinks lines. But instead of feeling dread, like the last time she was pregnant, she feels a sense of excitement.

She'd fallen pregnant 2 years before by her German lover, but as he was so much older than her, with 2 grown-up kids, he was not ever going to do that again—his words, not hers. Jodie did not want to be stuck in Berlin, a new business venture taking off and a single parent, so she had arranged for a termination. She does not regret this decision because it was not the right time, but now is the right time, and at that moment, Jodie realised she was going to be a mum.

She thinks about calling Jonny and telling him but decides not to. She doesn't want a relationship with Jonny; he's a player and, in her mind, not successful enough. No, she wants to raise the baby by herself. Jodie will tell Jonny at some stage but now is not the right time. She certainly doesn't want a conversation around having abortions. She will wait until she's past her three months before sharing the news. She also decides that her time in Berlin is ending, and she wants to go home to Australia. She starts to make plans to shut down Man Source and get the hell out of Berlin and back to the sunshine.

48

William and Jonny had been at one of Bree's many parties and had had a fabulous time. The night was getting messy with everyone tripping on pills, so they had both decided to leave at the same time.

After waiting for a taxi that didn't arrive, they had walked down to Chiswick High Road in the hope of flagging down a black cab and getting back to their respective houses. Both men were tired, coming down off the pills and in need of a joint and sleep.

After over an hour, William had managed to get the attention of a passing cabbie that was making his way back to Central London and accepted their ride to Hammersmith but did not want to go to Willesden for Jonny. William had offered for Jonny to stay at his place as he had a spare room, and Jonny happily accepted as he was desperate to get inside and relax.

Jonny is impressed with Willys flat and can tell that he earned well, just by the decor. They go into the lounge, and William pours them a whiskey while Jonny skins up a joint.

They talk for a while and listen to Pink Floyd, and at some stage in the night, Jonny must have fallen asleep on the couch because he wakes with William trying to move him from the couch and into the spare room.

To this day, they don't know who kissed who first, but they start to kiss, and before long, they are naked and having sex right there on the lounge floor. It doesn't stop there. They have sex in every room, and Jonny, much to his surprise, is enjoying it more than he wishes to admit.

'I knew you were gay,' says William while they are lying in bed smoking a spliff.

'I'm not gay, Willy,' Jonny protests.

'Well, if that wasn't gay, darl, I don't know what is,' says William, and they laugh.

Jonny ends up spending the whole of Sunday with William. They lunch, get drunk and stoned and have the best sex he has ever had.

When Jonny eventually leaves to go back to his house in Willesden, he is petrified his flatmates will guess what he's been doing, but he didn't need to worry. They just assume he has hooked up with a bird and has spent the weekend shagging her.

Jonny is confused. He knows he loves pussy, and he knows he's not gay. He swears blind he will never do it again, but right now, while he is lying in bed wanking, he is only thinking of William.

When he's finished, he feels ashamed and guilty, and for the first time in years, Jonny starts to cry. He promises himself he won't ever have gay sex again, and he won't wank off to thoughts of it, and if he pushes these feelings down, he hopes they will go away.

His phone pings to indicate he has a message. It's from William. 'Hey, darl, thanks for an awesome weekend. Don't feel guilty or worried and just so you know, I can't stop thinking about you.'

Jonny's stomach does a flip with excitement, and he goes to sleep thinking of him and wishing he were in William's bed right now.

49

Jonny and William have been a secret item for a few weeks now and it's slowly dawning on Jonny that he might be gay or the very least bi. The thought of never shagging another pussy is too hard to think about. Still, for now, Jonny is happily exploring the world of gay, and he's loving the attention.

William has been taking him to all the usual gay haunts of London. The attention Jonny has received has been mind blowing. His favourite place to dance is Heaven, where he and William have been regulars.

He's been very naughty lately, and on one occasion, William and Jonny were joined by someone they had met at Heaven, and the three of them had the best chem sex ever.

As Jonny is quite new to the scene, William has been taking it slow with him. William is madly in love with Jonny and wants him all to himself, but he also knows Jonny will want to experiment. He's not coming on heavy with him and giving him freedom but is also there for him at the end of every day. In fact, Jonny has practically moved in with him, and William loves it.

Jonny has been coming to terms with what has been happening. Though he hasn't told anyone yet, as he wants to see if this phase is just a phase or something more permanent. He is really enjoying the new scene he's fallen into. Back as a teenager, he'd had the odd snog with a guy while out in Cape Town, which he'd put down to the alcohol, but now when he thinks back, he realises that he had been suppressing these thoughts his whole life.

On the other hand, William wanted to shout from the rooftops about their relationship, but he's been sworn to secrecy and he doesn't want to run the risk of losing him. He couldn't help himself, though, when Jodie rang him a few days after coming to London and shutting down Man Source.

'Hey Willy, do you fancy catching up tonight for our goodbye dinner,' said Jodie. She had been in London for a couple of weeks. She still hadn't plucked up the courage to tell Jonny she was pregnant. She was flying back to Australia forever, just before Christmas and wanted to say goodbye to William but also had plans to tell Jonny on the day she flew.

'Sure, darl, but only if I can bring my boyfriend,' says William teasingly.

'Oh my God, I knew you had a man; you've been all happy and chirpy and so unlike you lately,' teases Jodie.

'Tell me more, what's his name?'

'Well, you are never going to believe who I've brought over to the other side,' continues William.

'Who?' demands Jodie.

'Wait for it, darl, it's the news of the century, I swear... Jonny,' says William.

There is silence on the other end of the phone, and for a second, William thinks she's hung up.

'Look, I know we shouldn't screw the crew, but it just happened, and I swear we didn't let it affect work,' continues William.

Jodie is still processing the news she has just heard, and her first reaction is to say, fuck off, you liar, but she's known William for years and knows he isn't lying.

'I have to say I'm surprised, William, but you sound happy. I had no idea Jonny was gay,' Jodie eventually says.

'Darl, he didn't even know he was gay, but you know me, I can sniff them out from a mile away,' William says jokingly.

'Ok, bring him Willy; it will be good to see him again.' Jodie's opportunity to tell Jonny had just come a bit closer than planned.

That night at the pub, after they'd ordered drinks and said their hellos, Jodie had congratulated the new relationship. She then dropped the bombshell, and it was Jonny and William's turn to sit there in shocked silence.

'Are you sure Jodie, you know, that its mine' offers Jonny a little apologetically, and William nudges him hard for being so rude. He knows Jodie, and she would never lie about something as big as this.

'Jonny, you are 100% the father, and yes, I'm keeping it before you ask.'

The only thing William is pissed off about is the fact that they had shagged without his knowledge but couldn't be mad because it had all happened before he and Jonny got together.

'Don't worry, Jonny, I don't want you, but if you want to be in the baby's life, I would love that and don't worry about money, I've got it sorted.' She must have read Jonny's mind because that's exactly what he'd been thinking.

The weirdest situation that could really happen turned into a joy and celebration that night. After the shock of finding out he was going to be a dad and the shock Jodie felt that her baby daddy was gay, they toasted the new changes in their lives. They agreed to be there for each other, no matter what.

'This might change where we live,' says William to Jonny that night when they are home.

'What do you mean?' says Jonny.

'Well, I don't think staying in London now is going to work for you if Jodie and the baby are going to live in Sydney. How about we head back there next year to support her?' says William.

'Would you do that?' says Jonny, who had been thinking about it since the news had broken.

'Yeah, I think it will be a good thing. Hey, we could even set up Man Source Down Under, just a thought,' says William as a passing comment, but Jonny likes the name of that, and they start to discuss their possible future down under.

50

And so, the day arrives that we have all been waiting for, 31st December 1999. For the last couple of years, the news has been full of stories of the world ending tonight as the clock strikes midnight and that the computers will be full of viruses. We will be waking to a new order. I'm not sure if any of this will come true, but right now, I don't care. We are getting ready to party hard, and the party has already started at my place.

Jess, Sam, and I have been dancing to music and snorting coke since 5pm. We'd been Pablo's 100th customer of the day. This is the busiest day of the year for him, so he didn't stop, only enough time to deliver the goodies and wish us all a Happy New Year.

I've put on the trance music I've been obsessed about since Berlin, though Oasis is still played between dance songs, and we've had it blasting for hours. We know the pubs will be heaving with patrons early on today, so we decide to stay at home before heading out to The Redback Tavern for the last time of this Millennium.

I'm still in shock at William, Jonny and Jodie's news, but the biggest shock is still Jonny. There were no signs, and my gaydar didn't go off once. I do sort of regret not shagging him. I'm sure I could have got him into bed if I'd given him the green light, but I suppose I should be happy to have them all as friends.

I spoke to Jodie last week on the day she flew home and thanked her for everything she had done for me and wished her and the baby the best. She's invited me to stay with her if I'm ever in Australia, which I plan to do at some stage.

I'm wearing my best fuck me dress and fuck me boots for tonight, and I don't care how cold it is out there. I have a skin-tight, silver sequined dress that sits just above my knee and is held up with two thin straps. My black boots end just below my knee, and I leave my long hair down. It's grown so long now it's almost touching my arse. I wear no knickers or bra. I feel like a sexy mother fucker, and I'm going to party like my life depends on it. As it's so cold tonight and we don't want to wear coats (and Jess is dressed equally as skimpily as me), we arrange for our cab to take us straight to the Redback from home. We want to get there early, so there is no line or a wait to get in.

The cab drops us off and there is no line waiting, just as we'd hoped and there are just four bouncers talking amongst themselves, trying to keep warm. They give us a smile and a nod as they know us well, and we enter The Redback Tavern for the last time this year. The place is busy but not crazy busy. The music is good and the band isn't due to start until 9pm. We have pills in our purse and grams of coke for the night, and we all know we are going to drop soon to get into the swing of things.

Everyone from Man Source has agreed to come in tonight and say hi, but as they are now two gay couples, I know they won't want to stay for long. Aggie & Smokey are the first to arrive. They look stunning and ready to party. They are off to a friend's house party later that night and will not be staying long. William and Jonny arrive next. They are quite pissed already. They have plans to go to Heaven a bit later in the evening, but they are happy to hang out at our table for now.

'We have some news,' says Aggie to us all once we are sitting down with our pints of snakebites.

'We got engaged this evening,' blurts out Smokey as she shows off her hand and the most exquisite diamond ring.

We all squeal with delight and congratulate them both. Aggie had got down on one knee this morning and proposed, and Smokey had said yes.

I go over to Aggie a bit later and tease her for being romantic, which she denies.

'Love is love, Bree, ya,' she had said in her usual dry tone, but she is smiling from ear to ear, and I know Smokey has somehow thawed her heart.

They leave after a couple of drinks and wish us all a Happy New Year.

'I hope the world doesn't end tonight' is Smokey's parting comment.

William comes and sits next to me for a chat. I get the feeling he's got something to say, and I wonder if he's about to tell me he and Jonny are engaged too, but it is something different.

'Hey darl, I'm setting up Man Source Down Under when I get back to Sydney next year and I'm going to need Consultants. How do you fancy coming to work for me?' he asks so casually that it takes a few seconds to sink in.

'What, you want me to work in Australia? With you?' I ask as I need confirmation before I jump off my seat in excitement.

'Yes Bree, I'd love to have you with me in my flagship company. You are quite good at what you do.'

'When do you want me?' I ask.

'I don't know, maybe February, March?' he continues. But I don't have to think about it and grab him hard for a hug whilst all the time saying yes!

'What's happening,' asks Jess, and I tell her about the job offer I've just had, and she says she's happy for me, but I can see she's sad too.

'Don't worry babe, it's only for a year. I'll get someone to rent out my room on a temporary basis,' but Jess isn't worried about that. She said she's going to miss me. We both start crying a little when we realise the enormity of it all. Sam cries too and comes in for a group hug.

'I'll call you in a few days, Bree, to work out the details. Have a wonderful night guys. Here's hoping the world doesn't end,' and he and Jonny leave to finish off their New Year's at the gayest club in London.

We've dropped our pills and we've all been dancing like maniacs for the last hour, though we are constantly checking to see the time as we don't want to miss midnight. However, the band has said they will count it down and then play Auld Lang Syne, so we don't have much to worry about.

The place is pumping, everyone is in good spirits, and the atmosphere is electric. The place is filled with happy, positive people, and it's really making the night, but then someone comes up behind me, puts their arms around my waist and starts kissing my neck. At first, I don't know who it is, and as I spin round, I come face to face with Juan. He is off his face on drugs and drink and can barely focus. He's falling all over the place and using me to steady himself. I push him away in disgust. He looks a mess. The friend he has come with is just as messy and I know the bouncers will throw them out soon if they are seen.

'Fuck off and leave me alone,' I say as I push him back into the crowd. I have no intention of being anywhere near this man ever, and especially tonight of all nights.

'Go back to your wife; you are a lousy husband,' I continue. He doesn't like what he hears.

'You're a cunt, and I was never going to marry you; did you know that, Bree?' he says spitefully, and the words hurt me, but I am determined to get away from him and not let him spoil my night.

Jess pushes him away, tells him to fuck off and guides me to the top bar. To our relief, he doesn't follow.

'Promise me you won't let that wanker ruin tonight, Bree, ok?' says Jess and I reassure her I'm ok but just need to be off the dance floor for a while.

The three of us stand at the bar watching the dance floor heave to all the good tunes being played and laugh as we watch Juan go from one girl to the next, trying to kiss them.

'What a fucking loser,' says Sam.

'Yup, a fucking loser,' says Jess.

'I'm so lucky I got away.'

And then we watch as a very fat and pregnant Charlene comes pushing through the crowd, having just been let in by the bouncers as they felt sorry for her after she'd told them her husband was inside. She was taking him home, red in the face from screaming and crying. The next moment she's dragging Juan by his arm and off the dance floor.

At this moment, I realise how lucky I really am to have got away and how I am now feeling sorry for Charlene, sort of.

With Juan off the dance floor and out of the Redback, it feels safe to return to dancing, and this is where we stay.

As promised, the band counts us down to midnight, releases balloons and confetti onto the crowds, and we all start to sing Auld Lang Syne. We kiss and hug everyone in the immediate area. Jess and I are crying from all the emotions and events that have happened over the last few hours.

'Your life is never going to be the same again, Bree,' says Jess as we finally walk to the front door to go home after hours of dancing. And I agree, it is never going to be the same again, and I'm excited.

'The world could have ended,' says Sam as we walk out onto the street.

But the world hasn't ended as predicted. Acton Town looks the same as when we left it a few hours ago. Cold and rainy with a million Australians, New Zealanders and South Africans milling around, trying to get home and Babylon Pizza Shop still serving up great pizza to all the drunkards out for the night. The place is alive and buzzing as usual.

This is Acton Town. This is my Acton Town. This is London.

Epilogue

A few weeks later. Thailand.

Jodie 'The Pikey' Lee - we were shocked to find out that Jodie and Jonny had shagged and that she is pregnant with his child. We think she had secretly hoped, deep down, that he'd want a relationship with her, but him coming out put a stop to that. She is coming to terms with the fact she is going to be a single mum and the father of her baby is gay, but it could be worse. She believes that Jonny and Willy will be great at parenting her child, slightly unconventional, but Jodie has never been conventional. She is back in Sydney now waiting for her baby's birth, which is due sometime in May.

Aggie 'The Slaggie' Swartz – finally found the girl of her dreams (even though, according to her, she was not looking) and has been living in engagement bliss with her once straight, gorgeous Israeli girlfriend. They have decided they want to be the first gay couple to get married once the laws change. I won't buy a hat just yet, but I look forward to celebrating their magical, historical day.

William Bentley aka Bent Willy & Jonny Rocks, South African stud muffin and Man Sources newest Gay!! Well, the shock and disbelief lasted for weeks. To be fair, no one believed a word of it until they started snogging like the lushes they are. All I kept thinking was, what a waste and I should have shagged him when I got the chance, Jonny, not Willy. They looked happy, and Jonny seemed surprisingly comfortable with coming out. Willy couldn't stop grinning as if to say, 'I told you so', and he had told me so all those months ago. There were times in the past when I had thought about it as Jonny could come across as very camp, but gay camp? I would never have guessed it. Yet here we are a few months later, and they are both going strong, living in Sydney's Surrey Hills, having a fabulous life and getting Man Source Down Under set up.

And what about little old me, Bree Jackson of Acton W3? Well, right now, as I type, I am sitting in a little internet café somewhere in Thailand, having travelled here to find myself, whatever the fuck that means. Sam and Jess didn't come with me as they didn't have the money and it was at such short notice, but they've promised to come to Sydney to visit. I realised I'd been in love with a first-class wanker, and I am completely over him. It's Charlene I feel sorry for. I genuinely do. Charlene and Juan had a baby girl named Aurora, and she's taken him back for their child's sake. I don't blame her; I'd probably have done the same.

I just hope he's stopped being a dick for the sake of his family. But a leopard never changes his spots, so I worry for the girls.

My 'find yourself journey' is almost at an end. I leave for Sydney in the morning. Willy has been hassling me to get my arse into gear and back to work.

I'm looking forward to it. I've had the craziest time here in Thailand; having just missed the Full Moon Party, I arrived at the world's biggest hangover, and it's been wild, wilder than Berlin and London put together.

So my travelling has come to an end, for now, though I plan to get back out there once my time in Australia is up. Who knows, maybe I'll stay. It all depends on how much fun I have. And guess what? I've met someone. Someone I think is quite special and we've been having the most amazing time and he's going to come to Sydney with me, and I'm totally besotted and excited, but hey, that's a different story altogether, just remind me to tell you someday.

About the Author

Charlie identifies as a human from Planet Earth. If you would like to contact Charlie, please direct all mail to 15 Yemen Road, Yemen or alternatively email info@charliepills.com

Disclaimer

This story is completely fictional as are the characters and events. If they sound familiar in any way, it is purely coincidence and it just means you partied hard in the 90's, shagged everything that moved, while taking a bucket load of drugs with people like Bree, Jonny and William. The places that are mentioned are real; the people and events are not.

Coming late 2022

Man Source
Down Under

by Charlie Pills

Printed in Great Britain
by Amazon

61489520R00183